A Cozy Country Christmas Anthology

by

Christine Arness

Published by
Melange Books, LLC
White Bear Lake, MN 55110
www.melange-books.com

A Cozy Country Christmas Anthology, Copyright © 2014 by Christine Arness

ISBN: 978-1-61235-980-9

Cover Art by Becca Barnes

A Cozy Country Christmas
Christine Arness

This book of Christmas stories is dedicated to my aunt, Dorothy, always a cheerleader for me, my family and my writing. I am blessed.

The Memory Tree

"Mom," asked thirteen-year-old Lynda, clutching a child-sized rocking chair, "What happened to the big box of ornaments?"

We were gathered in the family room to clear a space for the Christmas tree, and my heart ached at the answer I had to give to the four children staring at me expectantly.

"It went in the attic after Dad took the tree down," I explained, trying to control my own emotions.

"You mean it got burned up?" Six-year-old John's eyes widened. "Just like my rocking horse and bug collection?"

Krista, our three-year-old, burst into tears.

"Hush, sweetie," I soothed. "It's okay. Mommy's here."

The ravenous fire that consumed our farmhouse six months earlier had also charred the edges of the children's security. They grieved again at each fresh reminder of a lost toy or treasured token of childhood.

"We're safe," I reminded them. "All we lost in the fire were things. Things can be replaced. People can't."

"So we're just gonna have a bare tree this year?" nine-year-old David said with a frown. "Won't it look kinda funny?"

"The tree won't be bare, silly!" Despite his confident tone, Jon turned to me for reassurance. "Will it, Mom?"

"No," I vowed. "I thought maybe we could take a trip to town on Saturday and buy some new ornaments."

"Buy them?" Lynda cried. "We can't just go to a store and replace that box! What about other reindeer Grandpa carved when he was a boy? Or the snowflake Grandma helped me crochet when I was little? And that tiny green sled David painted when he was in second grade? We can't buy stuff like that!"

I rubbed the spot above my heart, trying to massage away the ache. Those ornaments had told the story of our family—how quickly they'd been reduced to ashes and soot.

"Now you made Mom cry!" Jon accused his big sister.

"I'm sorry," Lynda apologized, chastened.

"It's okay, sweetheart. That box was filled with precious memories, but we can't dwell on what we don't have. Let's be glad we'll be together to celebrate Jesus's birthday. Now, no more blubbering, all right?"

We worked until bedtime. When I tucked in the children, I got some extra big hugs.

"We have wonderful kids," I told my husband the next morning as we sipped our coffee. "Just call me blessed."

"If you can say so even though I was finally getting used to calling you Peggy." Doug dodged the piece of toast I tossed in his direction. He squeezed my hand as he headed outside to tackle the morning chores. "I know this is going to be a tough Christmas, honey," he said. "But we'll get through it."

"Together we can do anything." I squeezed his hand back. The ache in my chest was still there, however.

Soon, it was the weekend. To my surprise, none of the children wanted to come on the Saturday shopping trip I'd promised. "We've got something more important to do," Lynda informed me.

"A project!" Krista announced. She adored projects.

The Memory Tree

That afternoon as I walked in the front door, arms loaded with grocery bags—I couldn't help picturing the twin milk cans from my grandfather's farm. They had flanked the entrance hall in our old house. During the holiday season, they were always filled with evergreen branches, a woodsy scent greeting each visitor. I paused, missing them fiercely.

I blinked back tears. Then, to my surprise, I heard laughter in the family room. I followed the giggles and discovered Doug and the children immersed in a sea of paper, ribbon, cloth, modeling clay and sequins.

"We're making memories!" Jon exclaimed, holding up a paper plate splashed with bright colors. "This is a picture of my birthday picnic in a pasture last summer. See, here's Uncle Matt and the bonfire…"

Krista tugged at my sleeve. "I drew a picture of my kitty. Daddy's gonna hang it on the tree with a silver ribbon."

"No store-bought ornaments for us, Mom. We're going to have a memory tree!" Lynda smiled radiantly. "Daddy helped us cut one from the woods, and we're making things to hang on it—things that remind us of happy times."

A proud evergreen stood in the corner, its branches already decked with a few misshapen ornaments. One of them was a crocheted snowflake.

Lynda noticed me gazing at it. "I made some mistakes," she whispered, "Just like on the one Grandma and I crocheted together."

I hugged each of our children, then got down on the floor to make a few ornaments of my own. The ache in my heart was gone and in its place, I felt a warm glow of peace.

Homemade memories, like cookies, truly are the sweetest!

THE END

The Most Important Ingredient

"What's wrong, Mommy? You've got a big wrinkle on your forehead."

I stopped scowling at the cast covering my hand and forced a smile for four-year-old Becky's benefit. "Mommy's okay, dear," I assured her.

As okay as any busy farm wife and mother with a broken hand, I muttered mentally. Just three days ago, a cow had pinned my wrist between her hard skull and a concrete wall.

I was still adjusting to the cast. Already, however, I knew it would put a crimp in my holiday baking plans.

Usually, I baked for a solid week each December. Then I presented cellophane-wrapped, bow-topped dishes of delights to neighbors and friends.

Fragile Swedish lace cookies, rich toffee diamonds, paper-thin butterscotch crisps and round brown sugar drops were among my treasured family recipes.

This year, I wouldn't hear my husband's admiring whistle and customary compliment: "Anyone seeing these creations, darling, can tell you've got an artist's soul!" One toss of a Jersey cow's head had spoiled my most favorite holiday tradition.

Ed had been practical about the accident. "So we don't give cookies this year. Folks will survive," he'd said. With a sigh, he added, "But I will miss your help in the barn…not to mention those lemon wafers of yours melting in my mouth."

Seven-year-old Amy burst into the kitchen clutching a handful of envelopes. "Mr. Anders just brought the mail! He said he couldn't wait to sink his teeth into your cookies."

She frowned. "I told him you hadn't started baking yet. Christmas is in two weeks, Mom. When are you going to make cookies?"

"I'm afraid Mr. Anders won't be getting cookies this year, sweetheart."

"No cookies!" Army stared at me in disbelief.

I held up my cast. "How can I mix batter with this on my hand? I'm sorry, girls, we won't be making any cookie deliveries this year."

Amy flopped down on a kitchen chair and turned a woeful face in my direction. "But I told my Sunday school teacher I'd bring cookies next week!"

"No cookies?" Becky tugged on my sleeve. "No cookies for Pop-pop?"

"Grandpa will understand. So will everyone else," I declared. "I can't be expected to shape dough into wreaths with only one hand."

After a moment of disappointed silence, Amy brightened. "You haven't got one hand, Mom." She jumped to her feet. "You've got five!" Grinning, she held up both hands.

Becky—not quite comprehending—caught some of her sister's enthusiasm and held up her tiny palms. "I have five hands, too!" she chirped.

"Girls, girls, calm down," I insisted. "You have to understand— cookie baking isn't easy. It's grown-up work—"

I broke off. Suddenly, I'd remembered long-ago hours spent in Grandma Ella's kitchen, one of her flowered aprons tied around my little-girl waist. Her voice echoed in my mind. "What is the most important ingredient in a good cook's kitchen?"

The Most Important Ingredient

I glanced at the earthenware canisters that were arranged along the table. "Sugar? Flour?"

She gave me a grin and a shake of her head. "No, child. It's love. Love makes every dish taste special."

My two girls never had the privilege of knowing Grandma Ella. Now, her earthenware canisters lined my kitchen counters—a reminder of a legacy of love.

I laughed and bent down to kiss each sweet, pleading face. "Amy, get out the mixing bowls. Becky, please find the measuring cups and spoons. We've got some serious cookie makin' to do."

When Ed came in from his evening chores, the kitchen was a disaster area. The girls and I were dusted with flour and sticky fingerprints decorated the refrigerator and cupboards. Bowls, baking sheets and cooling racks covered every available surface.

A smile chased tiredness from his face as he took an appreciative sniff. "Mmmm! My nose tells me my girls must have inherited their mom's magic touch with cookies."

"Run and get washed up," I told the excited children. "Mommy needs to start getting supper ready."

Ed scraped a hump of dough off the nearest counter. "Looks like Mommy needs some help cleaning up," he observed.

With a rueful grin, I gestured toward a plate of misshapen snickerdoodles. "I doubt that anyone seeing these cookies would know I have artist's soul," I remarked.

Ed put his arm around my shoulders. "Maybe not, hon. But anyone could tell you've got a mother's heart."

I snuggled into his embrace, savoring the start of a wonderful, new holiday tradition.

THE END

If Wishes Were Horses

"Oh, Mom, isn't he beautiful?" Eight-year-old Kim trembled with excitement. "I've prayed every night for a horse for Christmas ... and here he is!"

"He" was an Appaloosa that had galloped up our lane, nostrils flaring, before stopping at the barn door.

My husband, Bob, led him into a stall and slapped the animal's muscular shoulder. "I bet this fella belongs to Sue Martin," he said. "This morning, at the feed store, she mentioned getting a barrel racer."

Kim vigorously shook her head, insisting, "He's my horse. God sent him!" Refusing to be torn even for supper from "her" horse, Kim remained in the barn, currying the mud-spattered coat with a 5¢ comb she'd bought at months ago at a farm auction.

I finally got Sue on the phone. She'd been driving around in search of her missing steed. Soon, she arrived with a horse trailer. "'Silver Dollar' just got spooked by a neighbor's dog," Sue explained. "Thanks for taking care of him."

Kim stood by silently as the clop of hooves on the ramp drummed an end to her dream.

I put my arm around the slumped, narrow shoulders in the faded pink parka. "I'm sorry, Kim. But, even if someone did give us a horse for free, we couldn't afford to feed it."

9

Kim shrugged me off, weary of hearing how the drought a summer ago had left us barely able to make ends meet.

Later, as she pushed around vegetables in reheated soup, I noticed a tear splash into the bowl. We sat alone in the kitchen while Bob finished chores.

"I know you're disappointed," I soothed. "Maybe next year…"

Kim stirred her untasted soup. "I need a horse now. You don't have to buy me any more presents for the rest of my life. I'll get a job to pay for his hay—"

"Kim, we can't afford new shoes for you and a horse needs two pair!"

She ignored my feeble attempt at humor. "Christmas is supposed to be when you get what you want," Kim sniffed. "And I want a horse!"

I sighed. "You have the wrong idea, darling. Christmas is when we celebrate God's gift to us—His Son. And the best way to do that is by giving to others."

Kim stared into her bowl. Platitudes were useless, I realized. At her age, she needed an example to which she could relate.

I touched her hand. "For my seventh birthday," I confided, "I wanted just one thing, more than anything in the world."

No response. I pressed on valiantly. "It was a china tea set decorated with violets—a complete set with teapot, cups, sugar bowl and creamer."

Grudgingly, Kim queried, "Did your parents get it for you?"

"They planned to. But then my little brother got sick, and his medicine was very expensive."

She scowled but I continued. "Later, an aunt gave me $5 for a present. I was thrilled, because I could buy the tea set!"

Uninterested, Kim squirmed. "I'm not hungry, Mom. May I be excused?"

"You know what, though?" I ignored her fidgets. "I didn't buy it.'"

Kim stopped half way out of her chair. "Why? I thought you wanted it more than anything in the whole world."

I nodded. "When my dad took me to the store, I picked up that set and imagined pouring tea for my dolls." Even now, I could still recall the thrill of clutching that box close to me. "Then I saw a baseball glove and remembered Andy lying in bed at home."

Sinking back, Kim really looked at me for the first time. "You bought the glove instead? Did Andy like it?"

My vision blurred and I swallowed hard, once more engulfed by the anxiety and grief of that long-ago summer. "Andy never got well enough to play, Kim. But he slept with that glove in his arms. That made me happier than any tea set ever could."

I saw the sparkle of tears in Kim's eyes before she darted out of the kitchen, leaving me to my memories...and the hope she understood the message I'd tried to convey.

On Christmas morning, Kim didn't once mention horses. She thanked us for her new parka and matching scarf. "Open this one next, Mom." Eyes shining, Kim placed a big box in my lap.

I ripped away the tissue paper and gasped. In the box was a child's china tea set decorated with violets—complete with teapot, cups, sugar bowl and creamer.

Bob gave me a puzzled look as tears rolled down my cheeks. "Kim dragged me to five stores till we found that. And now you're crying?"

I held the box close, exchanging a loving look with our daughter. "They're tears of joy," I explained. "Kim gave me what I wanted more than anything in the whole world."

THE END

Live as in Lively

Jeff broke the news over supper, mumbling through his macaroni and cheese.

"Don't talk with your mouth full, son," I reminded, at the same time removing baby Amy's hand from her applesauce. "What did you say?"

Jeff rolled his eyes and took another mouthful. "I told Mrs. Sims I'd bring the sheep."

"Sheet?" I queried. "A sheet for a costume? Are you going to be an angel in the Christmas play?"

My husband, Dave, harrumphed. Jeff's older brother, Lance, laughed out loud.

Jeff groaned. "Aw, Mom—we're not doing a play. We're gonna have a pajunk."

"A what?"

"A pajunk. You know—we're going to act out the manger scene. Mrs. Sims said we needed animals, and I said I'd bring the sheep."

Now I understood. "Oh, a pageant! That's wonderful, dear. You said what?"

Jeff sighed. "I said I…uh, we would bring the sheep."

Dave harrumphed again. And baby Amy knocked her dish of applesauce on the floor.

Next morning, the local newspaper had an announcement about the Live Nativity. Jeff was listed as a shepherd and animal contributor. I bought an armload of that issue of the paper and mailed them to out-of-town family and friends.

Jeff, usually a bit shy, strutted around with his head high…and spent hours grooming the three ewes he and Dave had selected from our flock.

The pageant took place on a very frosty Christmas Eve night. Jeff, Dave and Lance (who reluctantly agreed to don a fake beard and a bathrobe to help out) left early with the ewes in the truck.

By the time baby Amy and I arrived, quite a crowd had gathered in the fenced-in area on the church lawn. We found a place near the front of the large canvas tent, and though the flaps were still closed, I could hear bleats and brays—and giggles—coming from within.

Dave ducked out from behind the flap and joined me, mopping a brow that was sweaty in spite of the cold.

"How's it going?" I asked.

"They're just about ready to begin," he informed me. "Mrs. Sims is trying to get everybody posed. But the sheep aren't cooperating."

Just then, the tent flaps were drawn back, and an appreciative murmur ran through the crowd.

The crèche featured Mary in a blue robe, Joseph in a crooked beard, and a straw-filled wooden manger with a plump baby doll. Three wise men in cardboard crowns knelt in homage, and three bathrobed shepherds stood close by.

A charcoal-colored burro was tethered on one side of the manger, and our ewes—looking nervous—were huddled on the other.

The children held their rigid postures, with varying expressions of awe and wonder at the miracle they beheld. Two little angels with wire and gauze wings came flitting around from behind the manger, and when the shepherds knelt in unison, spontaneous applause rippled through the onlookers.

Tears filled my eyes, blurring the edges of the scene. Amy clapped her chubby hands and waved at Jeff and Lance. Her brothers' eyes remained fixed on the manger.

As Pastor Matthews read the Christmas story, the photographer from the newspaper captured the scene on film. But when he focused in on the ewes, I noticed one of them was hungrily eyeing an angel's wing and stretching its neck for a nibble. Uh, oh, I thought…

It was just as I feared! The surprised angel gave a yelp and dodged out of the way—knocking the other angel and one of the wise men off balance. The first angel tumbled down, wings fluttering. The donkey brayed loudly and pulled away, tipping the manger while the ewes bolted for the parking lot. Jeff took off in pursuit.

Lance sprang to his feet, tripped on his robe and fell on his face. He scrambled up again and, after a slippery sprint, made a diving tackle. A flurry of flakes followed. When the snow cleared, he was on his back, clutching the woolly ewe to his chest as the critter's legs pedaled frantically in the air. More applause.

Mrs. Sims, wringing her hands, cued the choir to begin a chorus of "Away in a Manger". After a moment, we onlookers joined in, and our voices quickly drowned out the commotion as the cast reassembled in the tent for the benediction.

The day after Christmas, there was a full page of color photos in the paper. I mailed out another batch, since the picture of Lance holding the runaway ewe was right in the middle.

Sunday night over supper, Jeff had a bulletin. "Mrs. Sims says everyone liked the pajunk so much we're gonna do it again next year."

Dave winked at me and smiled at Jeff. "Maybe next time you boys had better wear your track shoes," he suggested.

Jeff forked up some mashed potatoes. "No problem, Dad," he assured around a mouthful. "Mrs. Sims made me promise that next year I'd bring a camel!'

THE END

Let It Snow

"Smile! You love parties." Nathan put his arm around my waist. "You can dance all night, Sal. That's why I married you."

"I thought you married me because I could dance all night, rise at five a.m., sit on a tractor for nine straight hours and still had enough energy left to inoculate a batch of piglets."

"All I cared about was the dancing." Humming, Nathan waltzed me around the room.

I let him hold me close, but items from my lengthy "to do" list kept popping into my mind. The living room carpet needed vacuuming and Kyle had spilled cereal in the pantry. Farmland, farm houses and farm kids needed constant upkeep.

Nathan massaged my back. "The house looks great, but you don't. Relax, hon, this is just a family party. Everyone would be satisfied with hot dogs on paper plates."

"Well, I'm not! I want this evening to be perfect so the boys will have wonderful memories of a family get-together. I hate to cut this dance short, kind sir, but I have a thousand things to do."

My partner reluctantly released me. "How about a fire tonight, Sal? Everyone enjoys a crackling blaze."

"I agree. A fire in the fireplace is warm and welcoming, but it creates ashes and soot. We're having an elegant buffet, not a marshmallow roast."

"I love marshmallows!" Josiah piped up, beaming.

"We're not serving marshmallows," I informed my son crisply and turned to Nathan. "Try to understand, darling. This party is our family tradition and I'm doing my best to make it special. I want the house to look its best."

My husband gave me a hug and headed off to puzzle over a tractor repair problem, our three sons in tow. I sighed at the thought of the grease and grime connected with such a job—most of which would end up on the kids—and dashed off to attack the remaining items on my list.

I tried not to think about my husband's comments. I loved Nathan and my three boys dearly, but to me, Christmas wasn't just gifts and gaiety. The month of December was brimful of cleaning, decorating and baking in preparation for our annual family Christmas Eve party. I prided myself on the tradition of serving excellent food and encouraging lively conversation in a beautifully decorated setting.

But today a strange heaviness weighed me down as I fed the chickens and checked on the yearling colt. My head ached as I twisted cookie dough into candy cane shapes and iced the peppermint-fudge cake. When the boys—three baths and a freshly scrubbed kitchen floor later—started a duel using the branches of greenery I'd arranged on the buffet table, I sent them off to clean their rooms. Again.

Sighing, I massaged my throbbing temples. Was I getting sick?

I had just started to tie red and green ribbon bows around rolled linen napkins when the boys reappeared, bubbling with excitement.

"It's snowing, Mom!" Ryan exclaimed, nose and hands pressed against the window. He wriggled like a puppy. "Can we go out and play?"

"Please, Mom!" Josiah and Kyle chimed in. "We could build a snow fort. It would be so much fun!"

But I had a party to put on. I didn't have time for fun. "No! You'll make a mess and track in snow. Read a book or play a quiet game," I ordered. "I've laid out your good clothes for tonight."

Their faces fell and they trudged away, shoulders drooping, while I tackled the window Ryan had smeared. At this rate, I'd never be ready for tonight's festivities.

Before he left, Nathan had tuned the radio to a station playing carols. As I wielded a spray bottle of window cleaner, I heard the beginning strains of "Joy to the World".

"There's no joy in our house," I muttered, feeling woefully unappreciated.

Neither the boys nor Nathan understood that I was doing all this for them!

Then I paused, paper towel raised to wipe away the last hand print. What exactly was I doing for the boys? All of my fussing and fretting had taken the "merry" out of our Christmas. My perfectionism had substituted "stress" for celebration of the season. I gazed out at the steady fall of snow, my heart aching, and suddenly thought about my mother.

She'd been gone for over ten years and I still missed her so much. Somehow, each winter storm had a spell that enticed Mother outside. She reveled in snow, whether it appeared in the form of blizzards or flurries. I remembered watching her smile in peaceful satisfaction as flakes fell on her upturned face and powdered her hair.

Mother believed snow was a special gift from God. In her eyes, the singular pattern of each snowflake affirmed the uniqueness of each person, the individuality of us all. If anyone questioned her passion for the white stuff, she quoted Shelly, "I love snow and all the forms of the radiant frost."

I used my apron to wipe away a tear, recalling those Christmas mornings when my sister and I were awakened early by Mother warbling, "Let it snow, let it snow, let it snow!" Giggling with excitement, we'd jump out of bed and into our snowsuits. The three of us would hurry outside to build a snow manager and shape a baby Jesus to lay in it.

Then it was off to serenade the cattle with Christmas carols while helping Daddy with his barn chores. Afterwards, we tumbled into the heavenly warmth of the kitchen, our mittens soaked and our noses red with cold, where oatmeal simmered on the stove.

I blinked back more tears as I pictured that kitchen, cluttered yet cozy, with a scatter of boots and mittens lying in a puddle near the door. Mother's current knitting project usually shared countertop space with the my father's handwritten milking log and the squirrel-shaped cookie jar handed down from Grandma Ethel. We could hardly eat our oatmeal because we knew that after this wholesome breakfast, we'd open our presents while sipping hot chocolate and nibbling molasses cookies dusted with powdered sugar.

I shook my head in disbelief at my own blindness. How could I have imagined that I could improve on those long ago Christmas mornings with all my polishing and scrubbing? I wouldn't trade one of them for a picture perfect party.

I slowly put down the window cleaner and paper towels, realizing that I'd been trying to create a tradition by hosting a memorable party each year. But in the whirl of planning and preparation, I'd forgotten my past. Forsaken my family customs by leaving them locked away in memory.

But memories fade. Traditions die if they aren't continued. Abandoned, they have no choice but to melt away, like snowflakes in the sun. Lost forever. Heartsick, I pressed my lips against the child-size hand print decorating the cool glass. Instead of counting my special blessings, I'd wasted my energy in cleaning them up.

But it wasn't too late! Snatching up my "to do" list, I tore it into tiny pieces.

Outside, snow continued to fall. There was time. Time to continue a tradition.

Nathan entered the room. "Shall I get dressed yet? Or is there something I can do to help you get ready?"

I tossed the pieces of my "to do" list into the air and laughed as the confetti fluttered down. "You can start by making hot chocolate. Enough for all of us."

My husband blinked. "Hot chocolate? What about the buffet?"

"I've decided to serve hot dogs. We can roast them in the fireplace. A fire is so delightful when the weather outside is frightful."

"You've been listening to too many Christmas songs," a bewildered Nathan decided.

"But the weather isn't frightful—it's perfect!" I tore off my apron and gave my dumbfounded husband a hearty kiss. "Say, what carols do you think the pigs would enjoy? Our cattle always preferred 'Away in the Manger'."

Nathan laughed as, with a song in my heart, I hurried to find my precious children.

"Boys!" I hollered. "Get your snow pants and coats on. We've got some memories and some snowmen to make!"

THE END

One Midnight Clear

The click startled Tim out of his bleak thoughts. "Hey!"

Raising his right hand, he stared at the woman whose left was lifted in an identical gesture—and belatedly realized they were handcuffed together.

Ignoring the jostling of passersby, Tim had been studying a store window scene of children sledding. The windblown curls and smile of the littlest mannequin reminded him of his daughter.

But Amy was in Georgia this Christmas Eve with her mother, a faraway place with no snow, no sleds—and no father. Tonight Tim fancied himself a brooding, Scrooge-like figure and he'd even muttered a few "Bah, humbugs!" as he walked.

Standing outside the store, he felt isolated amid the hurrying people. They all had places to go and loved ones to buy for while he had no one. Nothing. *God, I'm so lonely!* his heart cried in silent prayer.

Wrapped in his sorrowful reflections, Tim had been only vaguely aware that a woman had joined him until he was jarred from his apathy by their bizarre linkage.

The metal lay cold against his skin. Tim's gaze travelled up the sleeve of his companion to eyes the rich brown of molasses above a mouth shaped into a startled "o".

"Am I under arrest?" Tim asked. He'd never heard of cops, even the undercover variety, wearing purple stocking caps sprinkled with snowflakes.

The woman didn't respond. She might have stepped out of the store window, abandoning her plastic children on the hill of fake snow, before freezing again into immobility.

"What's the charge? Loitering?" Tim raised his voice. What kind of game was this woman playing?

"But I didn't. And if I didn't and you didn't—" Awareness animated his companion's features and she whirled, yanking Tim around, too. "Charles Martin Hunt! Where did you get these?"

Tim realized for the first time that a boy stood just behind them, a child who held his body rigid in a defensive posture.

Her tone and the use of his full name apparently convinced young Charles that evasion would be imprudent. "In your bedroom." A gulp. "I was looking for presents."

A gal who kept handcuffs in her bedroom. Tim arched his brows, his interest captured, along with his wrist.

A flush dyed the woman's throat scarlet and she shot an apprehensive glance at the man beside her. "You know you're forbidden to snoop in my room. And why try them out on this poor fellow?"

A defiant shrug, but Tim noted the sparkle of tears in the boy's eyes. A crowd was gathering, with people staring more at their strange tableau than at the window display behind them.

"Do you have the key?" the woman demanded, only to be answered with another guilty, but still defiant shrug.

She glared at the culprit until the comical aspects of the situation caused her lips to twitch. "Charlie, you've come up with a doozy this time."

With a charming tilt of her head, she smiled ruefully at Tim. "How do you feel about going to a family party with a pair of lunatics?"

Half an hour later, Tim found himself sharing a seat on a bus. In that span of time, he'd learned that the woman's name was Ellen, her husband had been a policeman, and Christmas Eve was not the ideal time to find a place where handcuffs can be removed.

"My husband was killed by a kid high on crack." Ellen leaned over to breathe the words into Tim's ear, so that Charlie, crowded on her other side, couldn't overhear. "'I kept his badge and handcuffs as a remembrance for Charlie when he's older."

"Losing his father must have been rough on your son," Tim offered gruffly.

"Charlie misses David." Ellen looked down at her lap. "Holidays are difficult."

In her wistful tone, Tim heard the echo of endless, lonely nights spent in a home where joy and happiness had once dwelt. On impulse, he said, "This season has been difficult for me, too. My ex-wife recently moved to Georgia with our daughter."

Ellen squeezed his hand in sympathy. "You must miss her dreadfully."

Tim nodded. If he could speak without bursting into tears, he'd confess that he'd give anything to undo what he'd done.

What had his single-minded climb up the career ladder gotten him? An expensive, soulless condominium, a corner office—and handcuffed to a stranger on Christmas Eve. In pursuing success, he'd ignored the principles for maintaining a healthy marriage, and now he was reaping the unhappy harvest.

"Thanks for understanding." Ellen shifted and the handcuffs chinked musically. "Grandma Maria would be devastated if I missed the family party. After I put in an appearance, we'll go to my place and dig out the key."

Surprised exclamations greeted their arrival at the apartment which was their destination.

An elderly woman bustled up and threw her arms around Ellen. "Merry Christmas! Who is this nice person?" Her gaze devoured Tim.

"Finally took an old lady's advice, eh?'"

"'Yes, Grandma. But good men are difficult to find, so when I finally met another great guy, I made sure he couldn't get away." Ellen held up her hand, her sleeve falling away to reveal that the two of them were joined together.

The sight was greeted with stunned silence, broken by gusts of laughter, after Ellen explained their predicament. Realizing that his companion was dearly loved by those present, Tim sensed a general disappointment that he hadn't chosen to accompany her of his own volition.

The situation was totally crazy, but Ellen's extended family took both it and Tim in stride. Dinner was served buffet style in a kitchen crowded with people, casseroles, and an enormous punch bowl. Grandma led them all in prayer before presiding over the chaos, a smile wreathing a face as wrinkled as the raisins spotting the rice pudding.

With a plate of food balanced awkwardly on his knee, Tim laughed over the retelling of family holiday stories. He enjoyed watching the play of expression on Ellen's vivid face.

Tim had grown up an only child. If his mother were here, she'd be appalled by the shabby furnishings and disgusted by the loud voices and hearty laughter. She would have fainted if a child scuffed his shoes on the carpet, much less spilled punch as a brown-eyed tot did here tonight. But in this household, family reigned supreme, each person an integral part of a loving, complete picture of togetherness.

Eating a piece of pecan pie, Tim savored the warmth of Ellen's leg against his as they crowded together on the sofa. Looking up, he caught sight of Charlie, who was gazing at his mother with a sorrowful expression that tugged at Tim's heart.

Grandma Maria opened her presents, insisting as each package was placed in her lap that the giver "shouldn't have bothered." Tim applauded with the others when the wizened little woman opened Ellen's gift; a shimmering pink silk slip, and let out a squeal of pleasure. The back of Ellen's hand brushed Tim's as they tried to coordinate their clapping.

Ellen's perfume blended with the scent of the evergreen branches. She was so precious—and he had no claim on her except for the thin metal circles which temporarily linked them.

Suddenly, Tim felt like an outsider, doomed to be forever shut out of the warmth of family life. He bit his lip, murmuring an inward prayer for strength.

Turning to Tim with a smile, Ellen said, "I think we 'd better go so you can get on with whatever you were doing when we kidnapped you."

Their coats lay across their laps. Because of the handcuffs, they each had been forced to leave an arm in one sleeve. With the ease of long familiarity, Tim reached over to help Ellen pull her coat up and around her shoulders.

In the doorway, Ellen turned. "'Merry Christmas, everybody!'"

"Mom!" Charlie pointed upward, his eyes sparkling. "You're standing under the mistletoe!"

Tim knew his duty. "So we are," he said promptly and bent to place a tender kiss on Ellen's mouth.

He wanted to prolong the intimacy. The kiss must have betrayed his feelings—when they parted, Ellen gazed up at him in surprise. A delicate flush mounted in her cheeks.

Both adults were silent in the elevator, with Charlie yawning and heavy-eyed. As they walked toward the bus stop, the boy's feet dragged.

"Come here, sweetie," Ellen said. "I'll carry you.

"Let me." Tim boosted the child into his arms.

Charlie snuggled his head against Tim's shoulder in a gesture of complete trust. Above, the stars gleamed in competition with the street lights. Tim walked slower, pretending his lagging pace was due to his burden, but he didn't want the trip to end. This is sheer lunacy, he thought, his heart swelling, but I love it!

Ellen's home was in a modest neighborhood where houses were decorated with Santas, snowmen, and multiple strings of lights. Snow frosted the bushes; a wooly white cap covered each roof.

"Let's get Sleepyhead tucked in and then look for the key," Ellen suggested as she unlocked the front door. "I hope it's still in the box where Charlie found the handcuffs."

Tim nodded, looking at the evergreen standing in the corner with its popcorn chains, the candle in the window, and a nativity scene, all evidence that Ellen had tried to make this a normal Christmas.

"Are you happy, Mom?" Charlie asked drowsily as his mother tucked him into bed.

"Yes, munchkin." Ellen bent to kiss him.

Tim admired a close-up view of the sweep of dark hair falling away from the delicate nape of her neck.

"I knew he was the right one 'cause he smiled at the kids sleddin' in the window. I asked God to get you a really good present," the boy murmured obscurely and fell asleep.

Ellen closed the bedroom door behind them. "What was he mumbling about?"

Tim indicated their metal bond. "Me, I think."

She stared up at him, her lips parted.

"He sees how much you're hurting without David," Tim explained.

"When he saw us together, he must have decided I was just what you needed for Christmas. I guess he thinks I'm an answer to his prayers."

Ellen's free hand flew to her throat. "And are you?" she asked, her voice a mere whisper, her gaze downcast.

Tim cupped her chin with his free hand, gently compelling her to look at him. Somewhere downstairs, a clock struck midnight. By unspoken consent they kissed. Breathless, they reluctantly pulled apart.

"I'm glad God had Charlie bring us together," Tim whispered, smoothing back Ellen's hair. "I feel reborn. It's a miracle wrought by a very small Christmas angel named Charlie.

Tonight I met a woman whose loveliness of spirit makes me long to know her better. If someone handed me the key to these handcuffs, I'd throw it away."

"Christmas is the time for miracles. Grandma says so, and she's always right." Ellen's vivacious face sobered. "But as much as you hate the idea, it's urgent that we find the key and free ourselves."

Tim knew he was grinning like an idiot. "What's wrong with our present situation? I find it quite cozy."

Ellen laughed, a chime sweeter than silver bells. "I confess, so do I. But I also drank three cups of punch at the party—and my bathroom is definitely a one-seater."

Tim pulled her closer and kissed those adorably quirking lips, confident that both God, Grandma and Charlie would approve.

THE END

Star of Bethlehem

A Star and a tree. Such a humble request. The snow came to just above my ankles, fresh flakes powdering the shoulders of my coat. The memory of Jill's wistful brown eyes haunted me as I struggled to open the sliding door of the barn.

The calico cat with a crumpled ear, an ever gracious host, met me as I stepped inside. The cows were standing patiently in their stalls, waiting for the milkmaid and her pail.

I could visualize the noisy chaos within the house—my four children were making Christmas cookies, candy sprinkles and drops of icing decorating the floor, their faces, the tablecloth and, hopefully, a few of the cookies. Steven was supervising from a kitchen chair, his smashed leg in its bulky cast propped on a hamper, the leg which was responsible for keeping him from his winter job as a garage mechanic.

The chicken coop had been my first stop and as I spread the corn in the feeder, I had avoided looking at the heat lamps which would have to be run 24 hours a day in bitter weather. The heat lamps reminded me of the electric bill lying in the unpaid pile in the kitchen drawer.

Tonight was Christmas Eve and before going to bed I still had to put the yarn hair on Jill's rag doll, hem Donna's skirt and sew the buttons on the boys' shirts. Christmas Eve, and there was no tree.

I had broken the news to the children less than a week ago. The breakfast table had been the scene of a stimulating debate as to the placement of the tree and very little oatmeal was being eaten.

Jill waved her spoon in ecstasy, seeing inner visions of evergreen splendor. "I want a star on the tree. A pretty star like the one I carried in the Christmas play! Jesus was born under the Christmas star, you know."

I could wait no longer. Joining them at the table, I explained that we couldn't afford to buy a tree this year. "We can't cut down any of the trees Grandpa planted, can we?"

Four heads shook a vigorous "no". "But where will we put our presents?" Lars, age nine, inquired plaintively. "They always go under the tree."

"We'll find a special spot." No one smiled. "Please don't talk about the tree in front of your father, children. He feels terrible about being unable to work and I can't get a job because he needs special care."

My voice broke and Donna jumped up to put her arms around me. "We can string popcorn and put it on the spruce outside the family room window. That way the birds will have a Christmas tree."

"Lars and I can have fun making snowmen," Jeff chimed in.

Jill was silent, but a crystal drop rolled down the babyish cheek and plopped into her untouched oatmeal.

I was a failure as a mother—couldn't even supply a tree to put my homemade gifts under. A honk signaled the arrival of the bus and triggered a wild scramble for coats, books and mittens.

Wrapping a scarf around my kindergartner's parka hood, I kissed the tip of her nose. "We'll have fun this Christmas, Jill. Leave it to Mommy."

The brown eyes looked at me solemnly. "I'll ask Jesus for a tree and a star. The star is really for Him."

The silence in the barn allowed Jill's words to echo in my mind. The radio in the house had been playing Christmas carols and I switched the radio set on a shelf to the same station and turned it on, hoping to soothe my inner turmoil. A tree and a star. Jill prayed every night for Jesus to bring her a tree and a star.

If I couldn't supply a tree, would her faith be shattered? Seated on the milking stool, I leaned my head against the warmth of Buttercup's flank, and ran through a mental list of friends who would be happy to loan me the money. Steven's pride would be hurt, however, realizing as he did that it couldn't be paid back. The doctor, the hospital and the various utility companies all claimed first priority.

Dippy, part-Siamese, as his crossed eyes attested, rubbed his cheek against my leg and purred. He was waiting for a squirt of milk and I obliged. Opening his mouth wide, he gulped happily and licked off the drops which had spattered across his whiskers.

As I fed Fawn, I began to feel more at peace. The animals, the scent of straw from the loft and the manger I was filling with hay reminded me of a stable in long ago Bethlehem. Jesus was born in humble circumstances among the animals and grain because there was no room in the inn.

I froze, pitchfork upraised. No room in the inn? There was no room in my heart for Him, either. My worries about bills, the children and Steven had crowded out the love and warmth of the Christ Child. No wonder I stumbled from task to task with a heavy heart.

I found myself singing along with the radio, anxious to get back to get back into the house and enjoy the wonder and majesty of Christmas with my family; the tinsel and glitter now seemed unimportant—we had each other.

I poured some milk into a pan for the cats and wished them all a "Merry Christmas" before going back out into the falling snow, the lights form the kitchen beckoning me with their warmth and cheer.

Jill was very quiet during supper. Throughout the day she had kept checking the spot in the family room she had reserved for her "tree" in hopes that it had been delivered, but without success.

After the meal, Donna and I cleared the table and Lars brought the family Bible to his father for the reading of the Christmas Story.

Steven had just reached the point where the wise men inform King Herod, "For we have come to worship Him," when the strains of "Silent Night" became audible.

Jeff ran to the window. "Look, everybody! We've got carolers!" There was a scraping of chairs as his brother and sisters ran to join him.

The snow fell softly, muffling the sound of young voices. I opened the window and we listened as our visitors sang three more songs. Donna and Lars ran outside to invite them in for cookies and hot chocolate. Al Miller, a Sunday School teacher and a good friend, was the leader of the group and warned his charges to wipe their feet on the mat before turning to Steven.

"We brought you a surprise," Al said. "I sent some of the older boys back out to get it."

The surprise was a three-foot-tall evergreen set in a tree holder and decorated with construction paper chains and handmade ornaments. Jill danced around excitedly, stepping on people's feet and strewing cookie crumbs on the family room carpet as the tree was carried in in triumph.

Her cup of joy overflowed, however, when Al reached into his coat pocket and pulled out a star trimmed in glittering gold. "This belongs on top of the church tree," he told Jill. "But I thought it might be happier here for a few days."

He lifted Jill so she could place it on the top of the tree. The chatter of people in the kitchen rang in my ears as I stared at the sweet smelling evergreen.

Al grinned at my shocked expression. "My Sunday School class wanted to do something special for a family and I happened to think of you and Steven. They've been slaving away on ornaments and paper chains for a month—just as excited about their surprise as this little sprout seems to be." He nodded at Jill who was seated cross-legged before the tree, head tilted back as she gazed up at the star.

I managed to stammer our thanks and Steven pressed Al's hand fervently. At the door, our good friend stopped to slip an envelope into my hand. "A Christmas angel left this at the church office for you folks."

33

He winked and began shepherding his charges, who were making snow angels with Jeff and Lars on our front lawn, toward the SUV and the van.

I counted the bills inside the envelope. I would be able to pay the utility bills and there was enough left over for groceries.

The vehicles pulled out of the yard in a flurry of snow, snatches of "God Rest Ye Merry, Gentlemen" drifting back to my ears.

The falling flakes melted and mixed with the warm tears on my cheeks as I whispered, "Let nothing you dismay—remember Christ our Savior was born on Christmas Day."

I looked up into a haze of white, and although I couldn't see it, I knew the Star of Bethlehem shone over our house that night.

THE END

In For A Penny

When he first mentioned the weekend visit, Rob talked of going alone. Slipping into his role of a surgeon preparing a patient for the upcoming ordeal, his words flowed.

Like a distracted patient, however, Dorothy's hearing turned selective with only fragmented phrases washing over her: "Back before you know it"…"Only gone two days"…"We'll both feel better when it's over…"

"I'm going with you, Rob." Her firm tone silenced his unspoken protest.

After a moment of staring, eyes narrowed, he scowled, turned, and stalked out of the condo. Biting her lip, Dorothy accepted this retreat, although she still struggled every moment with the knowledge that he'd walked out on her emotionally months ago.

So she'd laid down an ultimatum and now they were trapped together in the car, with unspoken awkwardness separating them from their destination.

As the sun glinted without mercy off the windshields of oncoming cars, stabbing through the protection of her sunglasses, Dorothy wondered whether, when Rob said, "we'll both feel better when it's over," he'd been referring to this weekend, their marriage or the birth of the new life stirring within her.

"Tell me about your grandfather," she said, the words spilling out and sending ripples to disturb the silence.

Rob hesitated. With her intimate knowledge of his thought processes, Dorothy could almost see him marshalling his words into orderly statements as though setting a row of delicate stitches. She waited with outward patience, the sharp edges of her fingernails gouging the palms of her hands.

As her husband swung the wheel in a left turn, Dorothy's gaze snagged on his left wrist. Tanned, softly curling golden hairs, strong, but marred by the clinical precision of his TAG Heuer wristwatch. Her nails dug deeper—she'd been hoping he would leave it behind. The ever present symbol that time served as the master of their relationship stirred a faint nausea within her. She'd asked, no, begged, Rob to leave his watch behind on this trip.

"My grandfather isn't a guy you can peg into a hole. He's not someone comfortable in society and he's never had much money." The sting of the unspoken "unlike your family" echoed in Dorothy's head.

Another pause as Rob kept his gaze locked on the traffic ahead. "Ham's over eighty now and a widower."

The marriage counselor's admonition, "Pretend you're on a first date this weekend," jabbed at Dorothy. But communication between them had become a nightmarish blind date of walking on eggshells, fumbling for words and tense silences. She shared the blame equally but didn't know how to break the cycle.

Again, the sunlight highlighted her husband's capable hands as he maneuvered the Mercedes through heavy traffic spewing out of the city and heading north. A weekly exodus to wide-open spaces, one they'd never made. She continued to stare at Rob's hands. The hands of a healer, yet he refused to mend their marriage.

Dorothy yanked her thoughts off that gloomy track and launched another conversational probe. "What did Ham do for a living?" She winced. Her laugh sounded like a titter in her too critical ears. "I assume he's retired."

"Ham'll never retire, not completely." Rob snorted as a reluctant grin teased his lips. The car accelerated to move around a slower vehicle. Another moment, then Rob blurted, "He was a cowboy."

Dorothy hated the paper-thin defensiveness that coated his words, the subtle accusation of snobbishness. Then the import crashed in on her. "A cowboy?!!"

Her husband's studied attention to his driving left no room for her to maneuver. She blanked out her thoughts, determined not to let him win by getting angry and lashing back.

With one hand, she caressed her midriff. Such turmoil had to be bad for the baby. A baby scheduled to be born into a home so blessed with the material and yet so poor in the emotional. Would this tiny life be raised in a two parent home?

As the miles murmured beneath the tires, cushioned in luxury, Dorothy pondered the mysteries of a failing marriage. When had the first unhealed wound appeared? Rob's schedule as a top-level trauma surgeon kept them physically apart much of the time, while his exhaustion and nervous tension from bearing life and death responsibilities nearly every day isolated them emotionally.

Dorothy knew she'd helped to create this division between them, that he viewed her requests for a reduced schedule as criticism or her frustration, when rare evenings together were interrupted with intrusive pages, as selfishness. Counseling had enabled her to see his side of the story but since Rob had neither the time, nor the inclination to attend counseling, she stood alone in her self-knowledge. Nothing she'd tried recently seemed to bring them closer together.

Until this moment, she hadn't realized how much she'd staked on this trip as a salvage mission. Rob might be able to avoid her emotionally but this weekend they were stuck together physically, without the beep of the ever present pager to allow him to escape, for at least 48 hours.

Dorothy blinked and raised her head. She massaged her stiff neck and stifled a groan. Somehow, she'd dozed off and missed a view of some of the lakes and rivers that Minnesota bragged about on license plates and official websites. She'd also wasted precious hours of potential bonding. Her mouth felt dry and a faint headache tingled behind her eyes.

She looked around. Wherever they were at, the road had been damaged by yet another severe winter, and not even the Mercedes' suspension system could level out all the bumps. Luxury defeated by an overwhelming force. Just like their marriage.

Dorothy had grown up in what Rob had jokingly referred to during their courtship as "the lap of luxury." Holiday travel had been to glitzy resorts set on sparkling lakes where every need had been met with a smile. Places with spectacular views, everywhere you looked a vista of beauty.

Her parents had never vacationed in places like this backwater, she reflected, peering through the passenger window. When Rob told her where Ham lived, she'd imagined thick woods smelling of pine needles and "nature", not scrubby pines alternating with birches and tangled ditches that bloomed with orange, purple and yellow wildflowers. Or weeds, depending upon your viewpoint, Dorothy reflected.

After perhaps fifty or sixty miles, they passed through only the third town since Dorothy had opened her eyes. More small lakes, more ditches, more wildflowers. She found herself wondering whether the names of those plants could possibly be as a colorful as they were themselves, trying to imagine where the people who lived in the small houses set well back from the road could possibly work. No big box stores or fast food restaurants in this "neck of the woods", as Rob used to say.

Used to. She yanked her thoughts back to the countryside. A bird flew alongside the car and then veered off, vanished. What did birds do after they raised a family? Fly south, find a new mate? No, Rob had once talked about ducks and geese that mated for life. This curiosity directed at something other than herself and Rob felt strange, yet welcoming.

"That's so strange."

Rob jerked his head around to stare and Dorothy realized, too late, that she'd said the word out loud. "I meant strange that there's so little traffic on the road."

"I told you before that this isn't a vacation paradise. No one in the Twin Cities has ever heard of—"

"Sibley's Corners!" Dorothy interrupted him, pointing to a faded sign that announced their destination. "We're here!"

"Don't sound so excited." Rob gave her a wary glance. "I don't know what you're expecting, but…" His voice trailed away.

Dingy houses huddled closer and closer together as though wary of open spaces as the Mercedes rolled through the town. For the first time, Dorothy realized that it must have been a dry season here up north. Lawns looked patchy and brown, drowsing under the relentless afternoon sun. A too-thin woman in shorts and faded tee shirt watered a circle of petunias, the life giving liquid trickling from a hose that sagged in empathy with her shoulders. She watched the expensive car glide past, her face expressionless.

Two blocks past the woman, Rob swung the wheel and then slowed as he pulled into a narrow graveled drive. Switching off the engine, he dropped his hands into his lap. To Dorothy's surprise, she heard him draw a sharp, inward breath.

Was he afraid? Her smart, driven husband, who'd put himself through medical school and faced down her family to get her to marry him, looked nervous. He wet his lips, reached for his travel mug for another drink, his stare fixed on the small, shabby house.

Dorothy turned from Rob to study it, also. Peeling layers of various shades of paint gave it the look of a bag lady caught on the nightly news, an elderly woman bundled in layers to ward off the chill of a Minneapolis winter.

So small! The passenger door clicked open, breaking her concentration, and she struggled out, with Rob's hand to assist her, an impassive, courteous butler. The muscles of her back ached with tension and her temples throbbed.

With a flip-flop of nerves Dorothy realized, I shouldn't have come.

If Rob was trapped this weekend, so was she. No hotels in Sibley Corners, Rob had informed her, his lips white and head held high. "So much the better," she'd retorted. Yes, so much the better. . .

The sun beat down on her uncovered head; a wave of dizziness washed over her and she grabbed at the sleek, hot side of the car. Rob had disappeared.

As her head cleared, Dorothy turned to find her husband a few feet away, almost slouched in the shade cast by a pine tree, his hands in his pockets, his poker stiff spine relaxed. Bewildered by this sudden shift in Rob's body language, she started towards him, her expensive shoes crunching on the dried out needles. No grass, just sandy soil, burnt by the acid from the needles.

"Ham, this is my wife, Dorothy. Dorothy, my grandfather, Hamilton Forest."

Forcing a smile to her lips, she slipped off her sunglasses and extended a hand in greeting. As her eyes adjusted, her mental sketch of an ex-cowboy as lanky and laconic crumbled into dust and fell among the needles.

Her husband's grandfather appeared to be an elf named "Forest"— or was he a gnome? The top of Ham's head only came up to the top of Dorothy's chin, while bowed legs encased in ancient blue jeans and gnarled hands remained as the only outward signs of his former occupation.

Ham gave his grandson an enthusiastic hug before turning his attention to Dorothy. A startlingly deep voice boomed from that tiny frame, "Pleased to meet ya, Dorothy! You've lassoed a good man in my Robbie."

For a moment, she forgot her queasiness as she returned her host's smile. "Yes, he's quite a catch!"

Rob's swift glance and wary expression betrayed his feelings regarding her sincerity but his grandfather threw his arms around Dorothy and gave her a whole-hearted squeeze. Tears stung her eyes. Loving human contact after months of isolation. Her lip quivered and she bit it hard to maintain her composure.

Ham peered up at her. "I can tell by looking at her that she's a winner, grandson. As pretty as dogwood blossoms in the spring! We'll get along just fine."

Although Rob stood beside her, Dorothy sensed his subtle withdrawal, the shifting of his stance so their shoulders no longer touched. Ham continued to beam as he regarded his visitors.

"What are you working on, Ham?" Rob bent over a saddle draped across a board, poked at the piece of wood supported by four legs. "What's this called, Ham?"

"That's a saw horse, Mr. Town fellow." Ham picked up what looked like a can of shoe polish and a ragged piece of cloth from the seat of a lawn chair. "I'm doing my daily polishing." He stroked the saddle's dark, moist looking leather. "Takes a heap of elbow grease to keep leather as soft as butter. You have to keep at it each day or it dries out, could crack."

A saddle as an image for her marriage? Dorothy rubbed at the tension banding her forehead. Too simplistic. Stop grasping at quick solutions, real life isn't black and white, she told herself.

"Still known as Handy Ham?" Rob punched his grandfather's shoulder with a playful light touch. "I'll bet you keep busy."

"Do most of my work for free now, Robbie. Someone's gotta keep the widder women in fuses and mown grass."

A swarm of gnats suddenly appeared beside Dorothy, tracing invisible, cosmic patterns in the air, trapped in an endless cycle of futility. She choked back a laugh; on this trip she was seeing literary symbolism everywhere.

Ham noticed her grimace and jerked his head toward the house. "Come inside, children. It's hotter than a branding blaze out here!"

Fanning herself with one hand, Dorothy followed Rob inside. Her vision of staggering into the guest room and collapsing on a bed covered with a cool white spread while lacy curtains fluttered in the breeze faded at first glance.

An open door to the right revealed a miniscule bathroom. Turning, she glimpsed a galley style kitchen through a doorway. The presence of a lumpy couch and a card table indicated that the room in which they stood served Ham as both living and dining space. The air smelled of dust and heat. Tears gritted like sand underneath her eyelids. No room here for three adults to spend the night—it barely looked big enough for one.

Rob had been right, she wasn't welcome. Sibley Corners lacked a hotel or even a motel, he'd warned her, adding that Ham didn't have space available for guests. But she'd been so desperate, grasping at this last chance to catch and focus Rob's attention. . .

"Thanks for putting us up, Ham." Dorothy could tell by Rob's sidelong glances that the house was even smaller than he remembered it. "Are you sure we won't crowd you? Is there a motel within a few miles? We could call for a reservation, take you out to supper—"

"Nonsense! I'm pleasured, Robbie. Don't get much company. All the local widder women bring over casseroles and hand knitted scarves at the drop of a snow flake. Those gals don't count as company, act more like a pack of wolves circling a downed calf." He arched bushy white eyebrows and smirked. "But I'm still able to dodge and jump—so far I've managed to keep a ring out of my nose!"

Rob grinned and Ham flapped his hand. "Now, boy, and tell me about yourself." He turned to Dorothy and waved at the couch. "And you, Missie, just set and rest your feet. You must be so tired after travelin' from the Cities."

Rob and his grandfather seated themselves at the card table, leaving Dorothy marooned near the front door. She hesitated before crossing the dingy carpet to the couch where she was immediately sucked down into the quicksand of the stuffing. Her husband was already deep in detailing his daily routine to Ham, whose wizened brown face creased in a proud grin.

To disguise her intense interest in Rob's revelations of his days, Dorothy selected a magazine from the battered coffee table.

Stockbreeder's Journal! Faded black and white photographs of bulls interested her much less than the torrent of conversation spilling from her normally taciturn husband.

"So you call yerself a trauma surgeon, Robbie. What's that when it's at home?"

Rob gave a husky chuckle. "It's a fancy name for a doctor who puts people back together after they get hurt in accidents. Hey, my patient last Monday would have made you laugh, Grandpa. A big, burly guy, he told me before the surgery that he drives a diesel rig so he's never home."

Dorothy stiffened. The parallel seemed obvious to her—was Rob sending her a message with his choice of anecdote?

"—so this guy's in the habit of climbing up and perching on the roof to get out of range of his wife's constant 'bellyaching' about him being gone. So I asked him as he lay there in bed, his leg in traction, 'What happened this time that was different? Did you fall off?' And he said, 'Not until she beaned me with our son's baseball. Got something for a headache, doc?'"

Ham wheezed, his gusts of laughter threatening the stability of the card table that he pounded with a gnarled fist. "Bet you got a million stories to share with your wife each week, right, Dorothy? Must be tough on you with your guy gone so much."

Ambushed. She forced a smile to her lips. Rob never shared, but why should he when she had expressed so much resentment about his profession? She felt again the ache of having lost someone precious, the sting of throwing away something that could never be retrieved.

But Ham continued to beam at her. "But I suppose that's the life you two have chosen for yourselves. I can tell Dorothy's the strong, supportive type that she needs to be and, Robbie, you was a born doctor—'member your first patient?"

Guffawing, his grandfather hopped his chair around to include Dorothy in the conversation. "When Robbie waren't more than knee high to a grasshopper, he found this little bunny with a broken leg. T'was then he found his calling. He splinted the break and right away Mr.

Rabbit's sufferings were eased."

Dorothy felt her jaw sag, picturing Rob in his surgical scrubs, a frown of concentration on his handsome face, bending over a ball of fluff. "A rabbit?"

To her surprise, Rob's eyes sparkled as he met hers, before switching his grin to Ham. "Better tell her the rest."

"Oh, yeah, see Robbie had to use his brain box, didn't exactly have a medical kit, so he splinted that poor leg with stalks of rhubarb from his grandma's garden. The patient ate the instruments of mercy, so to speak, and hopped off. Never underestimate the curative powers of rhubarb." Ham bobbed his head, still chuckling to himself.

Dorothy yearned to keep the banter going, basking in the light in Rob's eyes when he'd looked at her. "Did he pay you in carrots?"

Her stomach roiled when Rob flicked an irritated glance in her direction, as if she'd intruded, thrusting in where she wasn't wanted. Somehow, in the past several months he'd managed to barricade himself behind invisible walls, leaving her standing outside, her fists bruised from pounding to be let in.

A sharp knock that brought Ham to his feet, the old man moving with the rolling gait of a sailor just off the ship.

After greeting the teenager clad in a faded red tee-shirt proclaiming "Mr. Quick's Pizza", Ham unfolded a bill from a roll tugged from his hip pocket and handed it over with an expansive grin. "Keep the change, Nicky!"

"Thanks, Ham." Nicky turned to include the visitors in the conversation. "My car knows the route here so well that my turn signal flips on all by itself."

"Quit yer kidding, sonny, and scoot, my company's chomping at the bit for a mouthful of supper."

Rob waited until the visitor had gone before asking, "Is pizza your meal every evening?"

He couldn't mask his concern and Ham's voice turned defensive. "I got this for a treat for you big city folks, Nicky's mom makes the best 'pie' in Minnesota. Hey, Nicky's just a kidder."

Greasy pizza and a can of generic orange pop served on a rickety card table didn't agree with pregnancy. Dorothy poked at the congealing slice on her plate while Rob and Ham caught up on family news. Ham kept trying to bring her into the conversation but for all the attention Rob paid her, she might as well have stayed at home.

She knew Rob felt guilty that he hadn't visited his grandfather since their marriage but did he have to take it out on her? Dorothy found herself frowning again and glanced up. Despite their proximity, her husband's gaze travelled through her as though her chair was empty.

With painful clarity, the finale from their last fight played on the mental screen inside her head. "You don't love me anymore—did you ever love me?"She'd spit those hurtful words at him, struggling to accept that he'd chosen an unending line of faceless patients over his wife.

Shivering, the memory faded to a dull throb at her temples. Glancing up, Dorothy saw Ham's deep-set eyes fixed on her untouched slice of pizza.

"You ain't et enough to keep a newborn calf steady on four hooves," he commented, forehead wrinkling into canyons. "How's Robbie gonna hug and chalk you at this rate?

"Hug and what?" Rob gave his grandfather a puzzled grin.

"If yer wife's healthy and plump, sometimes there's a little too much to get yer arms around in one go. So ya hug a little, mark your place with chalk, and keep hugging till you're done."

Rob pointed a long, capable finger at the remaining pizza. "Eat up, Dorothy. I'll never get that pleasure if you persist in starving yourself."

A fly buzzed at the window. "As if you even wanted to!" The words burst out of a deep well of pain inside Dorothy. Naked longing mixed with hostility quivered in the echo of her words against the bare walls.

Facing her husband across the cluttered surface of the card table, she read the truth in his refusal to meet her imploring gaze. He mocked her because of his conviction that her love had died, his belief unshakeable while he remained secure behind the barricade of indifference.

Flicking a stubby finger at a milk bottle standing sentinel on the sideboard, Ham barked, "That tone of voice'll cost you a penny, Robbie!"

To Dorothy's bewilderment, her husband rose and fumbled in his pockets before displaying empty palms.

With a sigh, his grandfather reached into his back pocket and pulled out a shabby leather coin purse. Selecting a coin with shaking fingers, he handed it over to Rob who strode over and dropped the penny into the milk bottle, its metal making a hollow clang against the glass sides.

Ham shook his head with a dissatisfied frown. "Now, now. You left out the most important part, Robbie."

After a brief hesitation, her husband bent to brush Dorothy's cheek with his lips, a cool, passionless kiss that burned and stung like a slap.

Maintaining a grip on her composure, she kept her gaze focused on the bottle, willing herself not to cry. The glass had a milky tint, as though through the years it had absorbed some of the liquid it was created to hold.

Ham bounced up and proceeded to clear the table by sweeping paper plates and napkins into a plastic grocery sack. When he'd finished, he dusted his hands together and beamed at his guests. "Who wants the first bath? Dorothy?"

Still struggling with her emotions, she attempted to hide her surprise. "Not yet, Ham. It's only six o'clock."

The sun seams shaped Ham's face into a walnut shell. It seemed apparent that the meal's tension hadn't escaped his notice; he clearly felt under pressure to provide some form of entertainment. "Ain't much to do after supper. We could listen to the ball game on the radio…get an ice cream…play poker?"

"I vote for ice cream." Rob already stood near the screen door, looking outside as if longing to escape.

"How about you, darlin'?" Ham turned to her, his smile anxious.

"Ready for ice cream!" Dorothy infused enthusiasm into her voice but she didn't want to go anywhere. She wanted to remain in close proximity with Rob, hoping to push him into betraying the anger underlying his polite smiles, opening doors for her, passing a slice of pizza. But she couldn't put Ham in the middle. Her mission this weekend seemed doomed to failure.

Hooper's Ice Cream Emporium featured high stools lined up before an old fashioned soda fountain that would probably cost a fortune to recreate for a movie set. Dorothy studied the chalkboard tacked up behind the fountain. A weekend special named "The Northern Lights" featured scoops of orange and green sherbet.

Ham introduced them to the other customers with pride as "my grandson, the doc, and his better half, Dorothy."

Dorothy's tummy had settled down but her back continued to ache. Since they were up north, she ordered the weekend special. Perched on a stool, she massaged sore muscles while studying the bay window fronting on Main Street. Spinning back to the counter, she touched the napkin dispenser, marring its shiny silver surface with a print of her index finger.

Their desserts arrived in moments and she closed her eyes as a spoonful of the blessed coolness melted on her tongue. Ham, who'd chosen a chocolate strawberry cone, was too busy licking for conversation. Rob had turned on his stool to chat with an elderly couple at a nearby table, bending to scratch their equally ancient cocker spaniel behind the ears as the dog lapped with concentration at a dish of vanilla ice cream.

The enormous wooden blades of an overhead fan provided a background hum as they sliced through the hot evening air. She felt as if she'd stepped into a colorized movie classic, where the tinkle of the bell over the door might signal the arrival of a young Mickey Rooney and Judy Garland dropping by for a malted milk.

Dorothy became acutely aware of the cracked leather of the stool as it chafed the backs of her legs, the sherbet melting into a muddle in the bottom of her cup and Rob's studied avoidance. He seemed comfortable here, as he'd never appeared in her world. She realized with a twinge of nausea that she'd never tried to live in his.

In contrast to her growing misery, her husband grew boisterous, harpooning Ham by blowing the paper wrapper off his straw and contributing an entry to the tall tale contest in session at the counter.

The winner of the contest, an unshaven man in overalls, was awarded a free refill of his milkshake. He repeated the story for the benefit of each newcomer. "No placee can beat this town for heat. Last night, Elsie had a craving for a snack. I went out to the popcorn patch, peeled back a couple husks, and filled a bowl with already popped kernels."

Ham punctuated the latest burst of laughter by sliding off his stool. "Got to get these young folks to home. Need their rest, being plum tuckered out from that fast city livin'."

On the stroll back to the house, Ham offered Dorothy his bed. A vision of the army cot she'd glimpsed earlier in the bedroom lent conviction to her refusal, which he accepted with ill-concealed relief.

"But you're my guests." His smile wavered. "I'm an old fool, never thought about where you'd lay your heads—"

"I'll handle the sleeping arrangements," Rob said, his voice firm. "Don't worry, Ham, we'll be fine."

Overhead, stars winked in the evening sky while the sounds of their footsteps punctuated desultory conversation until they arrived back at Ham's house.

Dorothy took up her host's earlier offer and soaked as much of her weary body as was possible in the tiny bathtub, tracing the hard water lines on its porcelain sides with her fingertip. Closing her eyes, she visualized the snatched, sweet moments when they'd made love while Rob was on the medical school treadmill, interludes that had dwindled into rare physical intimacy. By her continued insistence that she be

48

placed first, she'd only pushed him further and further away.

Her parents' wealth and social status must have birthed fears in Rob that he wasn't good enough, but she didn't realize the truth until her careless words uttered in frustration and loneliness had torn their marriage apart.

Plucking at the chain, Dorothy lifted the plug. Water swirled and gurgled into a cyclone shape above the open drain, a grim parallel to a marriage's destruction. She'd never realized it before but such images were everywhere. Dorothy sighed, realizing with a shiver that a degree in literature hadn't equipped her for anything but seeing literary references in everyday life.

Hoping Ham had already gone to bed, Dorothy slipped on one of Rob's tee-shirts instead of the negligee she'd planned to wear. Although Ham had bragged about "birthing more hosses, calves and puppies than there's tumbleweeds on the prairie," she didn't want the poor guy scandalized by the sight of his granddaughter-in-law's bare legs.

When she emerged, she saw Rob kneeling near the couch. "Ham didn't have any extra blankets so I went next door and borrowed a couple of sleeping bags."

He'd zipped the two together and arranged them on the floor. Turning out the overhead light, he joined Dorothy on the makeshift mattress. With an apology in his voice, he said, "Ham was so excited to know we were coming that he didn't stop to think about where we'd sleep. If Rose were alive, our every need would have been anticipated."

She heard a yearning in his voice and whispered, "Rose?" This was the first spontaneous remark he'd made in weeks, a light gleaming through a chink in the fortress walls.

Rob hooked his wrist behind his head. "My grandmother. A gal from a Boston family of bluebloods who somehow ended up on a ranch with Ham. But she was practical and according to Ham, she learned fast. Sounds like she handled all the details while Ham did the dreaming. But they were so close, so in love. I remember thinking as a little kid that my house would be like theirs."

49

His voice roughened and he hurried on. "They lived in a cottage on the other side of this town. After her death, Ham sold everything they owned and bought this shack. Everything in the other house reminded him of Rose."

Just like everything in their house reminded her of Rob, plagued her with bittersweet memories. The sachet of dried rose petals that she'd brought on this trip was the remainder of the two dozen roses, their stems bound in a silver ribbon, delivered the morning after she'd accepted Rob's proposal. It wasn't until months later she'd learned that her starving medical school student fiancé had pawned his winter coat to afford the roses.

Roses. Rose. Rob's grandmother had given up her life for her husband. What had Dorothy ever given up?

"It's your fault," she muttered to herself.

But Rob heard and misunderstood. "You mean, the baby?" He snorted. "Be spontaneous in your sex life, that's what you told me that marriage counselor said. Look where that got us!"

A child needs a loving, stable home, not the raveled strands that bound her to Rob. His indifference to the news of her pregnancy had shaken her belief that the dying embers could be fanned into flame. The only thing he'd done on this trip regarding her pregnancy had been a couple of curt reminders to drink the bottled water he'd brought, to remain hydrated.

Insects buzzed outside; she longed for a breeze to stir the curtain at the window. Marriage counseling had come too late, she realized with the heaviness of sorrow. Rob felt bound to her by the new life and not by love.

Although she could feel the heat radiating from Rob's body, the distance between them seemed so great he might as well be sleeping in Minneapolis. The last year of stifled and pent-up communication separated them. The air remained breathless; a faint whiff of mosquito repellant rose from the material beneath her cheek.

Rob grunted, gave a soft snort before beginning to snore. Had other women lain beside him and watched him sleep, stroked back the rebellious lock of hair which fell across his left eye after making love?

Dorothy longed to believe that infidelity was responsible for his remote gaze—she could fight back against another person. But she knew in her heart that Rob remained physically faithful to his marriage vows. The love and cherish part had been ripped from the service, however...

Unable to bear the proximity to her lost dreams, Dorothy got up with careful movements to avoid waking Rob and wandered to the front door, which Ham had left ajar after locking the screen door. Gazing out at the darkness, Dorothy tried to empty her thoughts and relax.

"What's wrong?"

At the sound of Rob's voice in her ear, Dorothy shied like a startled horse and his warm hands closed on her bare arms, steadying her.

"Everything okay?" he asked.

She knew he referred to the baby and wished for one moment that he cared about her. "Just needed to change position—"

Breaking off, she stared at the colors that spattered the night sky, dissolving and reappearing. "So beautiful," she murmured. "Achingly, gorgeously beautiful. . ."

"Why do you think they have a special called "The Northern Lights" at the cafe?" His breath, ice cream sweet, stirred her hair. "Rose and Ham enjoyed living here. Ham said they used to walk after dusk and dance along with the Northern Lights."

"How romantic," Dorothy whispered, her heart aching. She no longer wanted to force a confrontation but just wanted to turn and find that his arms were waiting for her.

For a moment, his hand cupped the nape of her neck and then it slipped away. "We'd better get back to bed. Such as it is." After a moment, he said under his breath, "I never should have agreed to let you come."

"So I wouldn't see your grandfather? Wouldn't tempt you to love me again?" But the words remained unspoken, a leaden weight in her heart. She stood until the lights vanished, wiping the tears away with the sleeve of Rob's borrowed shirt, before going back to join him on the sleeping bags.

This was the first time she'd ever touched one of these things. Rob used to enjoying camping out, loved the Boundary Waters, according to Ham's conversation this evening. But had she ever asked what he preferred for vacation instead of insisting they go skiing at a Vail resort? Couldn't she have offered to do those things with him?

Combined with her demands that he choose her over his passion for his work, she didn't need a therapist to tell her what went wrong. Unfortunately, none of the professionals seemed to have an answer on how to repair her marriage. Wishing she could travel back in time and take her newfound wisdom with her, Dorothy fell asleep.

Crackling static awakened her from a dream of dancing ice cream cones. A sheet covered her bare limbs. Tasting fuzziness inside her mouth, she realized the sounds came from the old Philco radio on the sideboard. Dorothy yanked the sheet up to her shoulders and, rolling over, she squinted through a curtain of hair at their host.

Ham sat at the card table, with his back to her and his attitude of intense concentration. When Dorothy cleared her throat, he spun around, cheeks burning, averting his eyes from her sheet-wrapped form.

"Up already?" Shoulders hunched, he addressed his words to the couch.

Rob groaned, stood, and twisted. Stretching, he rubbed the tortured muscles of his lower back. "Lying on your floor felt worse than bending over an operating table for ten hours, Ham. And where's that garbled static coming from?" He clapped his hands over his ears.

"Hog and cattle reports. I allus listen first thing. 'Bout time you was stirring. Let you sleep this long cause I knowed you was both tuckered out."

Draping the sheet toga fashion around her body, Dorothy bent to lift a change of clothes from her overnight bag, Her lips curved in a smile when a shrill whistle came from a bird outside the window and Ham hollered, "Don't mind him', he ain't whistling at your legs. He does that every morning to make sure I'm up."

She slipped into the bathroom to change. Dressed in shorts and a stylish maternity top, Dorothy came out in time to see Ham place two glasses of water on the card table next to bowls of cereal. Rob, shirtless, stood by the lumpy couch. Her husband's body was anything but lumpy! She swallowed at the sight of his lean, yet muscular abdomen. Delectable as a piece of gourmet chocolate—she wanted to touch him, stroke his supple skin and press kisses against the strong line of his jaw.

How could he not want her as well? She closed her eyes against the overwhelming pain.

Biting her lip, she watched Ham look over the table with the care of a hostess checking on the place cards. "I'll get your water in a minute, Robbie," he promised.

Rob pulled a tee-shirt over his head, the bristles on his jaw scraping against the cotton fabric. "Since we're having cereal, Dorothy and I don't need water."

"Suit yerself. This stuff's powerful dry without it."

"We prefer milk." Rob took the few steps into the kitchen and returned with a carton. Opening the top, he tipped it and something resembling a lump of cottage cheese slid out and plopped in the middle of Dorothy's bran flakes, sending them flying like dried out leaves in a gust of wind. Dorothy recoiled, gagging, from the sour smell arising from the bowl.

"Ham, this milk has turned!" Rob exploded, squinting at the freshness expiration date. "This expired over two months ago."

"Them little numbers don't mean much," Ham said with his voice defensive. Then he brightened. "Wait, we had that big storm last month, lots of thunder and flash. Lightning must have clabbered the milk."

It wasn't the lightning that had clabbered Dorothy's appetite. Choking, she ran for the bathroom.

After recovering, she and a subdued Ham sat on the couch while Rob cleared out the refrigerator, expressing scientific amazement over the variety of bacteria growing on the discarded items. Then he left for the nearest grocery store to stock up on food supplies and baking soda.

Dorothy's nausea had subsided, but Rob insisted she remain behind near the bathroom. His threats to hire someone to drive Ham to the store once a week, "if you can't make arrangements on your own" had sobered his ebullient grandparent considerably.

"Rob's just worried about you not getting the proper nourishment or coming down with food poisoning," Dorothy offered. "He's afraid that you're not taking proper care of yourself."

They'd moved outside in the shade, Ham seated in front of the sawhorse, his worn rag tracing circles on the aged darkened saddle leather.

"I know." He sighed. "Guess it's easier to order pizza than to fix my own chow."

A car rumbled by then silence. Ham dabbed his rag into the can of polish and shook his head. "Truth is, it's plum difficult to walk into a kitchen, any kitchen. Reminds me of Rosie."

"What specifically reminds you of Rosie, Ham?"

"A sink 'cause I can still see her washing up dishes. Pots and pans. She was allus rattlin' pots and pans, baking bread, flipping batter cakes for Sunday breakfast…"

Dorothy noticed the trembling of his gnarled hands and looked away, respecting his privacy. Plucking a blade of grass from the sparse lawn, she watched a ladybug stroll down the green gangplank until it descended to the ground with the dignity of a matron stepping off a bus.

"Why did you give up being a cow puncher, Ham? Cows started hitting back?"

His wheezing chuckles brought an echoing smile to Dorothy's face, but her thoughts were still centered on Rob. Why was she obsessed with breaking through her husband's protective reserve, attempting to force an

54

admission that he wanted to end their marriage? Just flogging a dead horse, as her host would say.

A bee zoomed past Dorothy's knee, trailing a buzz like a mini sonic boom, pausing to fuss around the purple cup of a wild violet.

"T'was hard to give up ranchin'," Ham said at last. "Riding fences, sitting up all night with a foal that's poorly, driving cattle to market. . . " A playful wink. "Hard to give up all that fun. But when Rose started increasing with our first, Robbie's Uncle Peter, Doc Baker, took me aside and said it would be a rough birthin'. No hospital within a hundred miles of our ranch. So I sold out for little more than buzzard bait."

Dorothy rubbed her knee, still stiff from a night on the wooden floor. Rob wouldn't sell his beloved ranch for her. He'd buy her a ticket and put her on the first train going back East. . . "How did you make a living?"

"Didn't have much schooling, but ranching had taught me how to shingle a roof and fix a water pump. Lots of folks too busy making money to potter around the house, so I set up shop and put my kids through college doing a little of this and a lot o' that."

His eyes crinkled as a soft smile curled his mouth. Dorothy guessed he was traveling back through time to a home populated with children, pets, and his beloved Rose.

"You know, I'll betcha we filled that bottle with pennies more times than a steer has burrs in its tail."

She blinked. "Are you talking about the milk bottle? Why did Rob have to put in a penny yesterday?"

"Family tradition, Dot. My wife and I started over, dirt poor, in a new town. Most days Rosie and I didn't have two cents to rub together. But the rule was no complainin' over rain squalls—we had to save our breath fer the gully washers!"

Dorothy coughed. "Gully washers?"

"Downpours that wash away the landscape and overwhelm a soul."

She felt her lips tremble and Ham reached out to squeeze her hand. After a moment, his age roughened voice continued. "As a reminder we was hitched for life, whenever Rose crabbed about toting water from the well or I turned up my nose at beans and cornbread three days running, we had to put a penny in the bottle and do somethin' nice for the other. In for a penny, in for a pound. The young'uns learned right quick that scratching at each other would short them a penny and they'd earn the privilege of making all the beds for a week. "

"What happened when the bottle filled up?"

His head nodded with the rhythm of age. "Treat money. The kids allus voted to buy double-scoop chocolate strawberry cones." Turning back to his saddle buffing, he ventured, "Are you havin' trouble with my stiff necked grandson? Fergive an old man's killed-a-cat curiosity, but I noticed a mite of tension between the pair of you, on the order of two mount'in lions eying each other over a plump goat."

Her fingers trailed over the age-softened leather. "Ham, how do you let go of someone who's already let go of you?"

"Death's the only final lettin' go I ever heard tell of." He rubbed with vigor, head bobbing with each swipe of his arm. "Love ain't a rope you kin just drop and walk away from. Strong winds make a house on the prairie look dingy. "

He paused to rub his forehead. "Look, sweet pea, Robbie's a proud man. If he don't see a fresh coat of paint on the house, he thinks it's all weathered away. You've gotta chip through the grime—show him that underneath the soil, the paint's still fresh and new."

Love likened to a coat of paint? Had she been standing back in awe of a fortress's strength when all that stood between her and Rob was a few layers of dirt?

After Rob's return from the grocery store, they packed a lunch and went for a drive to a nearby lake. Rob rented a small motorboat and went fishing with Ham while Dorothy remained in the shade and did some serious thinking. Not the yearning and regrets type of thinking but about what it took for Ham and Rose to keep their partnership strong.

The rest of the day and throughout the evening, Dorothy kept quiet, encouraging the flow of memories between Rob and his grandfather. They went out for ice cream again after supper and this time Dorothy stepped out of herself and talked to Ham's friends and neighbors. This time she tried the chocolate-strawberry cone. Ham winked at her.

She kept looking up to meet Rob's puzzled gaze. Each time, she offered a tranquil smile, and, instead of regrets, the lightness of hope bubbled inside Dorothy. No more hand wringing and sighing, she told herself. You're going to be a woman of action from now on. He's got to see it to believe it.

Cuddling next to Rob that night, she felt at peace as she traced the lines in the upturned palm of his right hand which instinctively closed around hers. He sighed in his sleep and she leaned in close, pressing a kiss on the corner of his mouth. He snorted, then smiled. She sighed but this was a sigh of contentment.

After a breakfast of bacon, eggs and milk that wasn't 'clabbered', they had a checker tournament that lasted until lunchtime. Dorothy spent the last half hour of their visit with Ham under the pine tree, rubbing the saddle with polish under his watchful eye.

"I'm sending you a cell phone, Ham, so I can talk to you while you're out here polishing," Dorothy said.

Rob nodded, his baffled gaze locked on his wife. "That's a great idea. We'll keep in touch at least once a week. And we'll be back. Soon."

"Make it before the snow flies, Robbie. I'll be knee deep in wider women, crocheted mittens and casseroles come winter."

After stowing the overnight cases in the trunk, Rob enfolded his diminutive grandfather in a gentle hug. "Goodbye, Ham. Expect us within the next month."

"We'd love it if you could come back with us for a visit sometime soon, perhaps stay for a week or as long as you'd like," Dorothy added.

Ham beamed. "Thanks for the invite, Dot. I just might take you up on it. Long as you got room for my saddle and my saw horse."

He bustled into the house before returning to present Dorothy with an object wrapped in a brown bag left over from yesterday's shopping trip. She felt the smoothness of glass through the paper and the rasp of a leathery palm.

"Don't forget the lovin' that goes with the givin' and may the rains wash the dust from yer home," he whispered, winked and gave her a smacking kiss on the cheek.

As a child, Dorothy remembered accepting a "blind man's dare", walking across unfamiliar territory with eyes closed, hands clenched behind her back. The memory of that excitement, coupled with the fear that at any moment she could trip and skin a knee or bump into an obstacle with the dare ending in disaster, rose up in her. The stakes were much higher now, the prize more precious than the cheers of her playmates.

On the trip home, she tried to relax as she watched the scenery glide past the windows, planning for the future, their future. Rob kept sneaking sidelong glances at her and she realized that she was no longer the desperate pursuer, but a mystery, and her relationship with Ham was something her husband could not get his head around.

She cradled her gift on her lap until they reached the outskirts of the city and moved into heavier traffic. With Rob distracted, she unwrapped the bottle and said a quick prayer.

As the car idled at a red light, Dorothy turned Rob's face toward her, smiled at his startled expression, and kissed him hard on the mouth.

He sat motionless. Then he drew a deep breath and tugged a penny from the pocket of his shorts. Leaning forward, he dropped it into the bottle, the metal of the coin ringing against the milky glass.

"Ham gave me that coin when we were out on the water. He told me that a wife wasn't a seed you could drop on the ground, walk away from and expect a bumper crop."

Dorothy gave a giggle and rubbed her stomach. "I'm growing."

In For a Penny

He placed his hand on her "baby bump" and then bent to kiss her. She met him with equal passion and they clung to each other until impatient horns of the other drives startled them apart.

As the car glided into motion once more, Rob chuckled. "That coin was the continuation of a wonderful family tradition, Dorothy. My way of saying that I'm definitely in for a penny."

"And I'm in for a pound." She felt her lips stretch into one of the biggest smiles of her life. "I hope our kids like chocolate strawberry cones as much as we do."

THE END

Breath of God

Betsey knew, without opening her eyes, she'd overslept. The sleepy twitter of birds in the trees outside her window had given way to energetic debate, indicating that they were well along with the business of their day.

She sat up. Sunbeams spilling across the hand braided rug confirmed her fear. She was late! She hadn't made breakfast; she had to get Erik up and both of them ready for school—

"Betsy!" Karl Swenson's shout silenced the birds and jolted his daughter out of bed.

Tangling her foot in the quilt, Betsy crashed to the floor. Wincing, she scrambled up and grabbed her dressing gown before rushing down the stairs.

Her father stood in front of the stove, glaring into the interior where a fire should be burning. The familiar fragrances of fresh milk and corn wafting from his clothing in place of the scent of coffee only served as an accusation to her dereliction of duty.

Betsy rubbed the sore knee resulting from her fall and hung her head.

"The stove is cold." Karl's thick accent emphasized his disgust.

"I overslept, Papa. I'm sorry."

"The chickens were making such a noise I checked and found out they hadn't been fed or the eggs collected." He pointed to a pail near the door, with brown eggs piled inside.

Betsy gulped and looked down at the floor.

"Are you sickening for something?" The dairy farmer took a step closer and peered at his daughter; the bushy, sandy brows which reminded Betsy of sheaves of wheat drew together in a frown. "Your eyes are as red as Mrs. Jeppson's Sunday hat."

"I had homework." Betsy blushed because she hadn't been doing schoolwork; she'd burned the kerosene lamp by her bed into the early morning hours and wept over the last chapters of Ivanhoe. The love story, so beautiful, had her tears watering the pages like spring showers.

"I have fed and milked the cows. I have a field of corn that needs to be picked. Is a man expecting too much to want food on the table when he comes in for his breakfast?

Six year old Erik, blonde and stocky like his papa, appeared in the doorway with his suspenders trailing to the floor and one shoe on. "Time for breakfast?"

Karl Swenson ignored the hopeful question from his only son. "School foolishness again keeping you from your chores. Clothes need washing. The bread box is nearly empty. Apples are rotting on the ground in the orchard. You stay up late and ruin your eyesight on books. I have no breakfast." His voice rose with each sentence.

Betsy bit her lip and kneaded a fold of her nightgown. Not just books—she had discovered magazines and several were even now hidden under her bed. Her teacher had encouraged her to borrow them, declaring they would open her eyes to the wide vistas beyond a Minnesota farm. A fascinated Betsy had spent hours studying pictures of faraway places.

"I'm sorry, Papa," she apologized again, scurrying to the stove. "I can scramble eggs now and I'll do the baking as soon as I get home from school."

Karl slammed his hand down on the oak harvester table. "You have no time for school. Things must be done around here, today."

Betsy almost dropped the iron skillet. "No school?? But, Papa, I have three more years until graduation—"

Her father's cheeks looked as ruddy as Mrs. Jeppson's Sunday hat. "No school!" He spat the words in her direction and stomped out of the house.

Her head pounding, Betsy ordered Erik upstairs to finish getting dressed and followed him up to get ready for the day. Back in the kitchen, she lit the stove and toasted bread. After they'd eaten a hasty breakfast, she set him to work sweeping the hearth and polishing the fireplace andirons with a soft rag torn from an old sheet.

As she cleaned the kitchen, Betsy wondered why she'd been so foolish. This wasn't the first time she'd neglected her chores, but she'd never dreamed of Papa becoming so angry. Her stomach ached at the memory of his declaration regarding school. Why had she stayed up so late last night?

As she got out the washtubs and lye soap, Betsy blinked back tears, her eyes burning from the strain of hours of reading by the kerosene lamp. Papa had a right to be so angry. A man needed a full belly to strip corn from the stalks by hand under the hot September sun.

Filling the tubs meant many trips to the pump in the yard. Anyone who did the laundry developed strong arms doing the washing and hauling water. With each pail she heated on the stove and poured into the tubs, Betsy felt as if she were drowning her dream of becoming a teacher.

With her mother gone, Betsy lost all support for higher education or even finishing high school. Papa had been indentured as a farm hand at the age of eleven when he arrived in America from Norway and had difficulty reading a newspaper in English. He didn't understand his daughter's passion for knowledge.

Betsy put the sleeve of another work shirt into the wringer and turned the crank. If only she hadn't neglected her household duties in favor of the glorious escape of reading. Now Papa would ban her

Saturday afternoon visits to the library in town and she would never get to finish the serial in her favorite magazine. A tear splashed into the rinse water as Betsy squeezed out one of Erik's shirts, remembering just in time that the buttons would never survive a trip through the wringer.

The clothes line stretched like a tightrope between an elm and a maple tree in the back yard. Papa and Mama had taken her to the circus once when it came to town. She'd never forgotten the winking sparkles on the performers' costumes and the scent of roasted peanuts. Her favorite memory, however, was hearing Mama's giggles and Papa's deep belly laugh at the clowns and their silly tricks.

She couldn't remember hearing him laugh since Mama... Betsy sighed as she lugged the basket of damp clothing and the tin can filled with clothes pins to the end of the clothes line.

Lefse, an orange and brown barn cat named for his exploit as a kitten of sneaking into the house and devouring half dozen of the flat pastries, wound around Betsy's legs and mewed complaints of starvation.

"You're plump as a market hog," she scolded him. "Go guard the grain and earn the milk Papa squirts into your mouth each morning at milking."

The thought of never going back to school gnawed at her like the sharp teeth of a varmint chewing through a feed sack. She stretched on her toes to hang a pair of Papa's work pants by the legs. The wind pounced and shook the pants as Lefse would shake a mouse to break its neck.

Lonesome for company, Erik wandered outside to join her. After rubbing Lefse's belly, he looked up and Betsy smiled at the black smudge on his nose. His eyes grinned up at her, blue as the autumn sky stretched over their heads.

He held up grimy hands. "My teacher will holler at me tomorrow for having dirty fingernails, Betsy. Can I play now?"

Erik thought they were enjoying a day off. With a pang, Betsy realized that Erik would suffer also from a lack of schooling. If they somehow lost the farm and a farmer was only one disaster away from doing so, her brother's only choice would be to work as a laborer for someone else. The breeze ruffled his straw blond hair and Betsy noticed that a button was missing from his shirt. She'd neglected both the house and her family.

Her brother stuck out his tongue and tilted his head back.

"What are you doing, you silly boy?" Betsy picked up the last shirt and a couple of clothes pins.

"Tasting the wind."

"And what does the wind taste like?"

He gave her a mysterious smile. "Just like apples and leaves and cinnamon."

Betsy stuck out her tongue too, but couldn't taste anything. Erik had such an imagination!

"And just a little bit like maple syrup." Erik loved maple syrup as a sweetener—in cookies and on oatmeal and everywhere he could get it. They boiled their own from the trees on the back quarter of their farm.

"You'd be happy if I'd let you drink maple syrup by the gallon." Betsy grasped the handles and lifted the empty clothes basket to rest on her hip.

Erik crouched to study an ant hill, grimacing when a gust of air kicked up a puff of dirt. He grabbed a sleeve from one of the shirts snapping in the wind and used it to wipe his eyes.

"Erik! That's clean! Or it was clean." Betsy's shoulders slumped when she saw that the black smudge of soot across her brother's nose had now transferred to one of his father's work shirts.

"Sorry, Betsy!"

She took down the shirt. "I haven't emptied the tubs yet—I'll wash it again."

"It's the wind's fault—it threw the dirt in my face, Betsy."

"We can't do without the wind." She ducked under the line of flapping clothes. "Without wind, how would the windmill turn? And the clothes wouldn't get dry. Mama always said, "There's no such thing as an ill wind—"

Her brother abandoned the ants and scuffed along behind Betsy through the long grass. "What else did Mama say about the wind?"

He sounded so interested, he always was when she slipped and mentioned Mama. But she didn't want to talk about their mother. Instead, Betsy dangled the basket by one handle and pretended the warmth of the sun on her shoulders was the touch of loving hands. But she'd already let Erik down today by antagonizing Papa about school.

"Folks say it's an ill wind that doesn't blow good to someone."

At Erik's puzzled expression, she forced herself to share a memory, one she kept locked away like a precious gem in a jewel box. "Even if the wind might not be helping us, someone else needs the breeze. I used to be afraid when the wind would howl on stormy nights, so Mama taught me a poem to help me be brave."

"Like Hickory, Dickory Dock?" It was Erik's favorite and as a little boy, he always checked their grandfather clock in the hope of seeing a mouse swinging on the pendulum.

Betsy paused on the steps of the washhouse and chanted:

"Wind is the breath of God ruffling our hair,
Changing the weather from stormy to fair.
Bending the grass and rustling the leaves,
Shaking the apples down from the trees."

Catching her breath, she remembered the last time she and Mama had picked up windfalls. They had been in high spirits, with Mama teaching her to juggle three apples and chasing her with a tiny green worm who had poked his head out of a hole. She blinked at the memories washing over her, the sweet smell of ripe fruit crushed underneath, the sound of wind tossing the branches overhead and the plop of apples dropping to the cushioning grass. Mother and daughter dodging between the gnarled trees amid the giggles of two year old Erik as he toddled around with an apple clutched in his baby hands.

Pressing her hand against her stomach, Betsy fought to hold in the hurt. For a moment, her mother had been there with them again and the realization that the happy time in the orchard had been part of their last day together brought hot tears welling up. Mama had been wrong, there were ill winds. One had blown across Betsy's life that day, one which four years later still possessed the power to dry up laughter with its scorching breath.

"Betsy?"

Erik's anxious voice made her manage a smile for his sake. "Papa missed his biscuits this morning. Help me finish the washing and then we'll take a picnic out to him in the field."

"Hurray!"

Like anything else on a farm, brisk breezes were not to be wasted. Erik helped his sister strip the beds and they carried armloads into the washhouse to soak in the washtubs.

Excited at the prospect of even a small outing, Erik worked hard, humming as he steadied the heavy flour sack so his sister could refill the canister. Betsy mixed bread dough and set it aside to rise. She sent Erik out to gather some windfalls. Along with the bread and biscuits, she'd bake a pan of apple crisp and a pie.

Mixing biscuit dough, she tried not to think about the future. Her brother arrived, panting as he hauled in the fruit. When he asked what he could do next, she asked him to get out the pie tins.

The sound of him poking around in the cupboard receded as she wondered whether she should have Erik start peeling apples. No, his skills weren't up to the task, but he could help cut out biscuits—

"Hey, Betsy! What's this silly thing?" The little boy held up a metal colander with a wooden pestle rolling inside.

She gasped and dropped her spoon into the floury mixture in front of her. Drawing a deep breath, she ordered, "Put that back, Erik!"

"Can I take the silver cone down to the pond and strain for frogs?"

"No!" Betsy jerked the colander out of his hands and whirled to replace it in the cupboard. Kneeling, she gazed blindly at rows of dusty, capped Mason jars that lined the long unopened storage area.

Sitting back on her heels, she gazed at the colander. Someone had cleaned away the applesauce. Closing her eyes, she remembered...

* * * *

Kitchen windows steamed from the fog of boiling water. Sara Swensen opened a window to allow the late September breeze to play peek-a-boo in her handmade organdy curtains.

Betsy stood on tiptoe to peer into the depths of a pot bubbling on the stove. "The apples must be mushy enough by now, Mama!"

"I'm raising such an impatient dumpling, Betsy. Apples have to be very soft before they can be made into applesauce."

"Can I measure out the sugar?"

Erik, his blue romper-covered bottom planted on the floor, clapped plump hands together to call attention to his successful stacking of two wooden blocks on top of each other.

Bending to hug her son, Sara praised, "Such a clever little man!"

Excited by the attention, Erik knocked over the tower with his elbow and burst into a wail of dismay.

His mother planted a kiss on top of his head. "Don't cry, my little potato cake. Build me a barn for Papa's cows."

As the baby chuckled over his handiwork, Sara poured softened apples into the colander. When it was nearly full, she inserted the pestle and began to roll the heavy wooden implement, crushing the plump fruit. Betsy stuck her finger into the sauce oozing through the holes and transferred the warm, tart mixture to her tongue, groaning in pleasure.

"Let me take a turn and smush the apples, Mama."

"Betsy, keep up the wheedling and you'll grow up to be a fine cook or a rich beggar."

Pushing a chair over to the table, Betsy stood as tall as possible as her mother triple-tied an apron around her waist. "Your mama's going to start fattening you up like a hog bound for market. You're as thin as a baby willow tree."

A leaf, red and gold like the windfalls in the pails, blew in the open window, skidding across the oil cloth before drifting to the floor. Erik jumped up to chase it with the eagerness of a kitten in pursuit of a bug, pouncing when the leaf came to rest against the dry sink.

Betsy brushed the hair out of her eyes with the back of her hand, crooning as the pestle rolled in her fingers. "Smush, mush, hush. Smush, mush, hush."

A bead of sweat rolled down, tickled the corner of her eye. The pots boiling on the stove made the kitchen seem as humid as mid-August. Betsy loved the hours spent learning how to bake, sew and clean, watching her mama scour the tiles so clean that they could eat off the floor if they had a mind to do something so foolish.

Mama made every moment fun, teaching Betsy to square dance using the mop and broom for partners or making up silly rhymes about why a pig's tail was curly or how daisies knew when it was time to poke their white bonnets up through the spring grass. And then there were those hours spent sitting in Betsy's room and making plans for her future. Serious talks about becoming a teacher, the secrets to making a husband happy and the joy of raising children.

While Betsy pressed the pestle against the metal sides of the colander, her mother used the tongs to place empty jars into a pot of boiling water.

"Always boil the jars, Betsy. They must be clean or you can make your family sick."

Every word her mama said during these magical times seemed to be written down in her mind in the beautiful colors of the Northern Lights, never to be forgotten.

Turning, Betsy saw her mother come in with her arms full of wood to replenish the supply for the stove.

As she brushed dirt from her calico apron, she smiled at her daughter. "Your papa has promised we'll have electricity one of these years and we'll also get a telephone. We'll get a radio, so on winter nights we can hear music from faraway places."

Her mother had come from a wealthy family in Minneapolis, enjoying the pleasures of gas lighting and graduating from a woman's teaching college. Instead of educating a group of children, however, her dreams had shrunk to teaching one daughter about the joys of knowledge and the household arts. But she had never expressed regret.

"Music from faraway places?" Betsy loved to dance around when her mother played the pump organ in the parlor. "Like St. Paul?"

Betsy's best friend, Libby Hanson, had moved to St. Paul to live with her grandparents when her father had been killed in a farm accident. The girls exchanged letters and Libby wrote about cable cars and picture shows. St. Paul sounded like an exotic country to Betsy.

"Music that your father and I can dance to." Sara swayed to an inaudible tune. "If we lived in the city, we'd have electricity, a telephone and a fancy bathroom."

Frowning, Betsy ignored the reference of to her parents dancing. "But we couldn't keep cats and cows if we lived in the city. And how could we make apple sauce without apple trees?"

A kiss pressed on the top of her head made her shiver with happiness. "Don't fret, my Betsy. We won't be moving to the city. Your papa loves this farm and I love your papa. We're very happy here. God even paints the sky for us with green and pink lights. We don't need a radio to have fun—"

Her mother's hug suddenly became a heavy weight on Betsy's shoulders and she winced away from the oppressive contact. Sara Swenson staggered away and leaned against the table.

"Mama!" Betsy started to climb down from the chair. "Your face is as red as Mrs. Jeppson's Sunday hat!"

That Sunday hat was a family joke. The widow had worn the hat to church as far back as Betsy could remember, a scarlet confection crowned with matching plumes that became more and more shopworn with each passing year.

Whenever Papa saw a cardinal, he'd say, "There's the bird who donated some of his feathers for Mrs. Jeppson's Sunday hat."

But this time, Mama didn't laugh and it made Betsy's tummy feel funny. The flush coating Mama's cheeks gradually faded, leaving her face bleached as white as Betsy's petticoat.

With unsteady hands, Sara Swensen used the tongs to remove the jars from the boiling water and set them in a row on the towel spread across one end of the table.

Papa had once told Betsy, "When your Mama's happy, even her voice smiles."

Betsy didn't hear any smiles when Mama said, "My head aches, Betsy, so I'm going to lie down for a minute. Add sugar to the applesauce and fill the jars. Please be careful not to burn yourself. I'll help you clean up the mess when I come downstairs. Please take care of Erik for me."

Mama rested her hand on the doorpost as she left the room and Betsy glanced at the windows to reassure herself that the sun hadn't disappeared behind a cloud. But it wasn't gloomy out there, just inside her heart. She felt queer, as if something fluttered in her tummy. Poor Mama. She'd been having these headaches more and more, spoiling their fun together.

But pride at having been given the responsibility to finish the final batch of applesauce took over as Betsy added sugar, measuring twice to make sure, and ladled the warm sweet mixture into the waiting jars. Erik had curled up on the floor and gone to sleep, one of the blocks that Papa carved still clutched in his fist.

Betsy wiped up the applesauce on the oil cloth covering the table and added the peelings and cores to the bucket of apple chunks destined to be fed to the pigs and the chickens. She decided to leave the colander, sticky and awkward, for when Mama came back to help her heat water to wash the supper dishes.

She punched down the bread dough that had puffed up so high in the heat from the applesauce making for the final time and covered the pans with a dish towel. When the fire died down a little more, she could pop the bread inside and Mama would wake up to the delicious smell of baking bread.

Betsy swept the kitchen and wiped off the dust on the window sill that had blown in along with the leaf. The kitchen had cooled down a little, so she went and got a small quilt to cover up Erik who was snorting like a baby piglet in his sleep.

Glancing at the clock, Betsy realized it was almost time to start supper. Why wasn't Mama up yet? She climbed the stairs and peeked in. The window was opened; Sara Swensen loved fresh air, breezes blew through every room of the house until autumn's chill took over. Betsy's mother curled up on the wedding ring quilt covering the bed, one hand tucked under her cheek. The other hand lay palm up beside her.

Betsy took the limp hand in hers. It felt cool and slack to the touch. At least Mama wasn't running a fever. Unfolding the wagon wheel patterned quilt at the foot of the bed, Betsy draped the comforting material over her mother and closed the window before tiptoeing back downstairs…

"Betsy!" Erik tugged her back into the present, yanking on her apron strings. "Why are you staring in the cupboard? Did you see a mouse?"

She placed the colander back inside and closed the door on the jars in their orderly rows and the memories. Knees aching from kneeling on the tiled floor, Betsy remembered her father's words from this morning, "Apples are rotting on the ground in the orchard." A ten year old could be forgiven for mistaking death for sleep, but Betsy still shuddered from the thought how she had failed her beloved mama when she needed her most. If only she'd gone upstairs earlier, perhaps she could have saved her.

Realizing Erik was gazing at her with a puckered expression around his mouth, as if deciding whether to cry, Betsy clapped her hands together. "Guess what! I've got a penny in my pocketbook for you to pay my big helper."

Her brother was quite willing to be distracted from the cupboard's contents and ran upstairs to get his bank. Betsy checked the oven before cutting out biscuits and arranging them on the baking sheet. Erik arrived, puffing, clutching his bank, which was made of iron and very heavy.

He watched her until she wiped her hands on her apron and fetched the penny. Grinning with excitement, he placed the penny into the dog's mouth. With a whir, the iron canine jumped through the hoop held by a man in a bright red jacket and deposited the coin into the barrel on the opposite side of the bank.

Laughing in delight, Erik hopped up and down and Betsy found herself smiling, yet envying his joy. If only finding happiness could be as easy as putting a penny in a bank, but a hundred dogs jumping through a hundred hoops couldn't bring back her mother.

When the biscuits were done, Betsy wrapped them in a napkin along with cold tongue and a chunk of homemade cheese. She accompanied Erik down into the root cellar and let him fish out juicy pickles from the brine in the pickle barrel. A couple of apples and a jug of buttermilk completed the picnic lunch.

On the walk to the field, Erik skipped ahead, darting to chase after a brown rabbit and flapping his arms to imitate birds in flight. They found Papa giving the mare a drink from the bucket he carried on the back of the wagon. Grundel, the black and white dog who always followed him around the farmstead, lay panting in the shade of a huge hickory at the end of the field, a tree whose roots always reminded Betsy of enormous bent fingers clawing into the earth.

Karl Swensen straightened while Erik raced forward and wrapped his arms around his father's knee, which was as high as he could reach. "I want to play in the corn, Papa!"

After being lifted into the wagon, Erik picked up two ears of corn and tried to juggle.

Betsy cleared her throat. "We brought your lunch."

Her father turned towards her and she saw the weariness carved in the lines of his broad face. "It's a good time to take a break."

Neither of them spoke while they ate, Karl nodding at Erik's chatter and only smiling when his small son offered to turn a somersault.

When they finished, he plucked his red bandana from the pocket of his dusty overalls and wiped his mustache. "Good biscuits, Betsy."

"Please take care of Erik for me." Her mother's last words echoed inside Betsy's head, drowning out the chirp of the birds in the hickory tree and the rustle of the corn leaves. She clenched her fists and said in a loud voice, "Papa?"

He turned from soaking his bandana in the water bucket to look at her, his eyes the same clear blue as Erik's, the blue of the sky.

"Please, Papa, don't blame school, it's my fault. I stayed up late reading, not doing school work. I promise to take care of the house and I understand if you won't let me go back to school, but you have to let Erik go. He must have the chance to learn." Betsy set her teeth into her lower lip and pinched a fold of her calico skirt.

Karl mopped his brow. "With your hair pinned back, you look like your mama, Betsy." Typing the damp cloth around his sun-tanned throat, he sighed. "Sara wanted you and Erik to get an education—book learning was very important to your mama."

"I miss her very much." The words squeezed out of Betsy's throat.

Her father closed his eyes. When he spoke, his voice sounded gruff with emotion. "I'm sorry. I shouldn't have bellowed like a bull this morning—you've done a woman's work for the past four years and you've done a good job raising Erik."

Words of praise. Betsy couldn't imagine any of her friends' fathers apologizing to their children and her voice sounded husky in her ears, "Thank you, Papa."

His hand, thickened and scarred by years of toil, squeezed her shoulder with gentle pressure. "A man must acknowledge his faults, Betsy. Your mama would take a broom and shoo me back from the gates of heaven, if I told her I took you out of school." He nodded. "You and Erik have fun this afternoon because tomorrow you're going back to school."

Betsy rubbed Belle's rough mane and the mare blew through her nostrils. "Maybe we should get Belle a straw hat on our next trip to town, Erik. A red hat, as fine as Mrs. Jeppson's Sunday best."

Erik, convulsed with giggles at the thought of the horse wearing a hat with feathers, had to be told twice that it was time to go back to the house.

As they walked away to the jingle of Belle's harness, the wind made waves in the long silky grass which bowed around their feet and the relentless motion, combined with relief that Papa hadn't banned school, made Betsy dizzy. Erik tried to sing the song she'd sung to him earlier, but he could only remember the line about the wind shaking the apples down from the trees.

"I like to eat the apples God shakes down from the trees, but I'd rather throw them. Will you play under the trees with me, Betsy? I promise not to throw at you as hard as I can." He flexed his arm to show his muscles and then looked disappointed that his shirt sleeve didn't bulge like Papa's did.

Betsy hadn't set foot in the orchard since Mama died. But the trees held a great attraction for Erik, who loved to stalk the cats with pocketfuls of little green apples for ammunition.

Memory suddenly slanted white hot light into a chink in the darkness of the cupboard with the colander and the dusty jars. Mrs. Nelson, the neighbor lady who stayed with them while Papa fetched the doctor, must have washed it.

Betsy didn't remember much about that day after Papa had run down the stairs to tell her that Mama was dead. Forgotten until now was what she'd overheard Mrs. Nelson telling a group of ladies at the funeral.

But now those words jumped into Betsy's head, along images of black armbands and the sounds of sobbing.

"The poor young woman had put up over a dozen quarts of applesauce before she took sick. The children were outside when I got there, the babe chewing on a twig and watching his sister hurl jar after jar against the house. Broken glass everywhere and fresh made applesauce dripping down the boards. Child didn't even seem to realize what she was doing—"

Betsy stopped to gaze at their house. For a moment, she could almost see the white paint marred with brown streaks.

As if it were happening all over again, the pain crushed her chest, tears blurred the grass as she carried out shining brown jars, the sound of breaking glass delighting Erik into laughter. Clanging pot lids together his new favorite game, he loved loud noises.

"I broke them because I thought making the applesauce killed Mama," Betsy whispered.

She blinked and the memory of the brownish streaks vanished. Dropping the hamper, she ran forward and pressed her nose against the sun warmed boards. She sniffed. Not a hint of apples. Papa had repainted the house and never mentioned the incident. Never asked her to make applesauce, one of his favorites.

Only then she realized the colander had been sitting in the cupboard for four years, ready for use. The pain eased as Betsy remembered the rolling motion of the pestle in her hands, the pride of wearing a woman's apron, even if it had to be triple wrapped around her waist, and the leaf dancing across the yellow oil cloth, blown by the breath of God.

Erik collapsed, stuffing the last biscuit into his mouth while a blue jay hopped closer, hoping for crumbs. When her brother beamed at her, Betsy felt a rush of love, as warm and rich as new made applesauce. She stooped to kiss the top of his tousled head.

When Erik tossed the rest of the biscuit, the bird snatched up its prize and sprang into the air. Together, they watched the blue jay land on a tree branch.

Breath of God

The breeze hurried the clouds along overhead and blew against Betsy's forehead in a gentle benediction. "The breath of God ruffling our hair," she murmured.

"Let's go pick up the rest of the windfalls, Erik, and you can help me make applesauce this afternoon. We can have a fight but you must promise not to throw as hard as you can."

He jumped up and turned a somersault, sprawling on his back and giggling. Betsy laughed, too, as overhead the blue jay fanned out his wings and launched itself into the waiting arms of the wind.

THE END

The Piano Christmas

If Sara hadn't left her lunch pail behind, she never would have seen Miss Ellen wrapping the Christmas presents—a pile of gleaming glass balls at on the rickety wooden table Miss Ellen used as a desk. Peeking through the open cloak room door, Sara watched her teacher's deft fingers wrap an ornament in a flannel square and tie up the bundle with ribbon. String for boys, hair ribbons for girls.

Sara tiptoed out of the schoolhouse door and hurried down the snowy path, the memory of the spheres gleaming in the lamplight warming her like a flame.

Christmas *Eve* was tomorrow and Sara knew Miss Ellen set great store by gifts—the teacher often related stories about her family Christmases back home in Boston. Sara's favorite tale concerned the holiday referred to as "the Piano Christmas". On that morning, Miss Ellen had discovered a grand piano, wrapped in a giant satin bow, standing next to the Christmas tree in the drawing room. But Boston and such lavish gifts seemed as far away as Europe to Sara. The only present she received last year was an orange after the church Christmas program.

Sara found herself skipping in her clumsy boots. Mama would scold for being late; after supper, the women planned to decorate cookies to hang on the tree Papa would cut down tomorrow,

As the oldest in a family of seven, Sara was kept busy at mealtimes. Tonight, however, Mama had to ask her three times to pass the dish of pickled beets because Sara couldn't get her mind off the pile of glass balls on Miss Ellen's desk.

Over and over, she pictured her family admiring a tree decorated with popcorn strings and gingerbread men. Sara, stepping forward, would hang her ornament on the tree, the sparkle of the glass in the firelight making the room brighter.

"Oh, Sara! Where did you get it? It's beautiful!"

Her brothers and sisters would gaze at Sara with awe in their eyes as she explained, "Miss Ellen gave it to me."

"What are you mumbling about, child? I declare, you must have left your mind as well as your lunch pail back at that school you're so fond of."

Grandma's sharp voice penetrated Sara's happy vision and she realized she'd spoken out loud. "'I'm sorry, Grandma. Just excited about Christmas."

Mention of Christmas sparked a memory in Krista. "Will I get an orange tomorrow?"

"Don't spoil the surprise for your little brother and sister," Mama replied, cutting another slice of bread for Eric.

Curled up beside Krista that night, Sara licked a bit of frosting off her hand and thought about her present. A crystal globe was much more exciting than a scarf or mittens; Mama had been doing a lot of knitting lately.

Sara's ornament was bound to be the most beautiful. Wasn't she Miss Ellen's special helper, in charge of leading the Pledge of Allegiance each morning, buttoning up the smallest children's hobnailed boots, and reading aloud to keep the class quiet when Miss Ellen stepped out?

Out of all fourteen children in the school, Miss Ellen definitely liked Sara best. Sara uttered a sigh of pure contentment. This was going to be her very own Piano Christmas.

On Christmas Eve, Sara had only half a day of school and she had as much trouble sitting still as seven-year-old Anna did. But Miss Ellen kept them busy; each child was set to working on a present for his or her own parents.

Sara chose to draw a picture. Studying the portrait of her family at dinner, with Baby Karl perched on a catalog and Papa carving a roast goose, she decided the drawing lacked something and added a tree in the corner. A tree with popcorn chains, gingerbread—and a glass ornament.

A shadow fell across her picture.

"What a silly present!" Jimmy, the bane of Sara's life since he'd dipped her braid into an inkwell and made up a silly song about the gap between her front teeth.

"I found a rock to prop the barn door open when Dad's carrying in water for the cattle," Jimmy continued. "That's a real present."

"Why don't you just use your head for a door prop? It's as thick as a rock!" Sara retorted in a fierce whisper.

Jimmy scowled and Miss Ellen, who was helping David make a pen wiper, looked up. Sara ducked her head and pretended to draw. She didn't want Miss Ellen to hear her squabbling with Jimmy.

Jimmy walked up to the front of the room and used the dipper to get a drink from the water barrel. Out of the corner of her eye, Sara saw his hand jerk and the water spill.

In September while chopping wood, Jimmy had severely cut his arm with an axe blade. Now his right hand twitched and quivered like a frightened rabbit. Some of the children made fun, getting their own back on a boy who had delighted in teasing them. But Sara never laughed. The sight of his twitching hand reminded her of the livid scar and wasted muscles concealed beneath his shirt.

Just before noon, Miss Ellen had the children clear their desks and brought out a tin of homemade fudge. Smiling, Sara watched the little children lick chocolate off their fingers before wiping her own hands daintily on the skirt of her brown pinafore.

Dressed in a dark red skirt, Miss Ellen stood in front of the room, her beautiful hair the color of chestnuts tied back with a wide red bow.

The students quieted as she began to speak. "I've had a wonderful time teaching you, children."

Sara sat with her hands folded primly in her lap. The others thought the fudge was their present—just wait!

"I wanted to get you something special, something you'll treasure for years to come."

I'll treasure my glass globe, Sara thought. I'll wrap it in cotton batting, store it in my trunk, and the ornament will be a family heirloom, like Grandma's mirror from Norway. My grandchildren will ask where I got the glass ball and I'll tell them all about Miss Ellen and this Christmas.

Miss Ellen looked as excited as Sara felt. "My sister bought your presents in a store in Boston. The package arrived this week and not a single one was broken during the trip!"

Sara stifled the urge to chew her thumbnail. She was tired of copper pots, iron stoves, and woolen stockings—she longed to own something exquisite and fragile.

Miss Ellen lifted the flannel wrapped packing from a string shopping bag. The last to receive a gift, Sara held her breath as she untied the knotted pink ribbon. What if the glass had cracked? After all, Jimmy had been tramping around the front of the room in his clumsy boots...

Sara sighed in relief. The glass ball was cold to the touch, but warmed under her palms. The sphere was perfect—more beautiful than she'd imagined—and seemed to glow in the winter light. Inside the fragile bubble sparkled a five-pointed star.

A crash stilled the chattering voices, and Sara whirled in her seat. Jimmy was the focus of all eyes, his own once delicate ornament reduced to powdered glass now sprinkled on the rough boards and across the toe of his boot.

His hand twitched. In a voice as harsh as a bullfrog's croak, he asked, "Can we fix it? I was gonna give it to Mom."

Miss Ellen shook her head and got out the broom. Jimmy began sweeping up the mess, his head bowed. Miss Ellen watched him for a moment before walking over to Sara's desk.

Sara breathed the sweet lavender scent of Miss Ellen's perfume. She felt sorry for Jimmy, but found it impossible to be sad for him and happy for herself at the same time.

Now Miss Ellen was going to say something nice, maybe thank Sara for all her help during the year. But instead of the expected compliment, the teacher's words struck Sara like a handful of icy snowflakes borne on the winter wind.

"Could you give Jimmy your ornament? I'll write my sister and ask her to send another one. You're my special helper, Sara, and I know I can ask you to be generous."

Sara's fingers tightened protectively around her treasure. Miss Ellen was asking too much. Give up her gift? Her voice was thick. "Will the new one be here by Christmas?"

She didn't want a new one, she wanted hers. The one with the star.

Miss Ellen's voice was gentle. "I'm afraid my sister won't even get the letter for several weeks."

Sara glanced at Jimmy. His injured hand trembled again and she looked away. She needed this ornament to hang on the tree tonight. She shook her head.

Miss Ellen smiled, but the light had gone out in her eyes. Squeezing Sara's shoulder lightly, she moved away.

Suddenly words burst out from deep within Sara, "Jimmy can have my ornament!"

"Are you sure?" The music was back in Miss Ellen's voice.

Sara nodded dumbly, wincing as Miss Ellen plucked the ornament from her hand and carried it over to Jimmy. Miss Ellen had been cruel to ask such a sacrifice. Winking back tears, Sara pleated the flannel square which had wrapped her ornament; the sweet aftertaste of the fudge charred to ashes in her mouth.

The other children giggled as they left, clutching ornaments and the presents for their parents. Jimmy carried his ornament, Sara's star ornament, in his good hand. He hadn't even said thank you.

Disappointment sat cold and heavy as Jimmy's stone door prop in Sara's stomach. She waited until the last child had been booted and each stray mitten collected before picking up her drawing and going to the cloak room.

Miss Ellen stood in the doorway. Sara didn't look up, feeling betrayed by her idol who had asked more than Sara was willing to give.

Stepping in her dainty, high-buttoned shoes, Miss Ellen walked over and studied Sara's drawing, which lay on the bench, the picture showing a table laden with food, the happy family members, and the tree. A tree on which a crystal globe sparkled, sending rays of beauty throughout the room.

Suddenly, Miss Ellen's arms were around Sara, enveloping her in the scent of lavender. "Oh, darling Sara, I had no right to ask such a sacrifice. Can you forgive me?"

The icy rock in Sara's stomach melted away as she returned the hug. "I don't even like Jimmy," she confessed and they giggled together.

"Thank you, Sara." Miss Ellen's voice was choked up, as if she had a cold.

Sara suddenly remembered her gift to Miss Ellen—weeks spent fancy stitching a handkerchief. In all of the anticipation of receiving her ornament, she'd forgotten it!

"I forgot your gift at home, Miss Ellen," she confessed.

The teacher chucked Sara under the chin. "You've given me the best gift anyone could want, chickadee. I'll treasure this Christmas always."

"Even more than the year you got the piano?" Sara asked breathlessly.

"Your generosity to Jimmy is worth more than any instrument, Sara.

A gift doesn't have to be store bought or tied with a satin bow to be very special."

On the way home, Sara leaped over drifts with the agility of a deer. She had a picture to share with her family. She'd given Jimmy—even if he was a tease—a present and still had the anticipation of another ornament from Boston for next year's tree.

The warm glow which had vanished when her ornament was taken away had been rekindled inside Sara's heart. Miss Ellen had given her respect—a gift which would never tarnish or shatter, a gift Sara could treasure forever.

This was truly a Piano Christmas.

THE END

Pocketful of Love

The yellow duck was so lifelike that Wanda wouldn't have been surprised to hear him quack. Humming "Away in a Manger", she poked the needle through white cotton cloth. The holidays wouldn't be quite the same without snow, but Wanda was a survivor: she'd learn how to make do with sunshine and the bright blue skies of Arizona.

The phone rang. Placing the embroidery frame on the coffee table, Wanda rose, wincing as her arthritic knee took her weight. The pain accompanied her into the kitchen like an ever faithful dog.

She had long ago decided that answering the phone was the biggest adventure left in her life. The caller could be Gwen inviting her out for lunch, an announcement that she'd won one of those jingle contests she was always entering, a salesman, or—

"Mother Wanda?" The voice was cultured and confident.

Biting back a groan, she responded with the warmest tone she could muster. "Hello, dear. How are you this beautiful morning?" Too late, Wanda remembered her daughter-in-law never stooped to answering personal questions, no matter how harmless or well meant.

"I'm calling about Christmas, Mother Wanda, and I've decided to be blunt."

Someday, her daughter-in-law was going to cut herself on that sharp tongue, Wanda mused, opening the cupboard door and reaching up for a tea bag. "It's an open line and an open ear you've got, dear."

"This year, David and I don't want homemade gifts." A shiver like an electric current ran through Wanda's body, but Allyson didn't hesitate before plunging on. "We prefer money. We have a long list of things we'd like this year. David's been looking at new flat screen TVs, I need a new carry-on bag for our upcoming trip to Hawaii—and I'd rather you bought the children's clothes instead of making them."

Wanda, stunned, clutched the tea bag until it popped and tea trickled like dark sand onto the floor.

The hurtful voice continued. "Jenny's in fourth grade now and what child wants to go to school in a homemade dress? If you don't know which designer labels are hot, just give me the money and I'll pick out the clothes myself. Now, I know David doesn't want you upset over this issue but be assured we are in basic agreement. Mother Wanda? Are you there?"

Wanda took three shaky steps over to the sink and turned the tap on all the way, the noisy waterfall splashing into the kettle, giving her time to regain her composure.

When the teapot was full, she murmured, "Thanks for sharing your thoughts, Allyson. I'll be sure to keep your suggestions in mind."

"Now you're offended." Allyson was the one who sounded miffed. "I'm making a legitimate request. We'd rather have money than embroidered hankies and homemade clothes. Family members should be honest with each other about things that matter."

Wondering whether Allyson's idea of honest would be to tell a woman on her death bed that wearing a brighter shade of lipstick would improve her looks, Wanda hung up the phone.

Trying to pretend that the call hadn't happened, she placed the kettle on the stove and turned up the blue flame. The canisters on the shelf rattled as she walked heavily to a straight-backed chair and sat down.

A vision of the work table in her bedroom imposed itself over the yellow and white checked cloth. She saw the twins' undershirts just finished, Patrick's embroidered with a blue lamb and Stephanie's a yellow duckling. A much larger shirt had the words "Dynamite David" and a tiny bowling ball and pins cross-stitched on the pocket. Daffodil bright, Jenny's skirt provided a light-hearted contrast to the drama of an evening cape shot with glittering silver threads made for Allyson. Each stitch represented a stab of pain—but Wanda's stiff, aching fingers had been impelled by love.

Wanda remained seated until the impertinent whistle of the tea kettle penetrated her gloom. Pouring the steaming water into a mug, she recognized the cup as the one David had given to her years ago; the crooked letters "M O M" had been painted by a boy who, when he concentrated hard, stuck out his tongue and scrunched up his eyes.

Picturing her son as a child, Wanda's heart overflowed with memories. Precious memories. She treasured the mug because David had struggled to shape the letters in art class, tied the straggled bow on the handle with awkward fingers, and beamed as he presented his gift. Such pleasure couldn't be found in a store or bought with a plastic card.

"Now, don't let that silly, young woman get you down," Wanda rebuked herself, addressing the remark to the glassy-eyed rooster cookie jar which served as her centerpiece this week. "She means no harm, just hasn't learned yet how to tell the difference between fool's gold and the real McCoy."

Despite her brave words, Wanda was still depressed when Gwen showed up on her doorstep several hours later, unannounced as usual, and waving an envelope of pictures taken at the Fit and Fifty talent show last week.

Her uninvited guest immediately accepted the offer of a cup of tea and sank into a kitchen chair, a watermelon pink skirt swirling around her shapely ankles. Wanda put the kettle on again, placed a cup and saucer on the table, and thanked her friend for picking up the photographs.

"No trouble, Wanda. I just finished showing a house two blocks away to a nice, young couple. Your pictures turned out great—I already took a peek."

Wanda fumbled with the flap of the envelope. "Rip up all the ones of me hula dancing," Gwen instructed, tapping the table with a fingernail tinted to match her skirt. "They make me look like a forty year old."

"So now cameras take twenty years off your life? I should look so good!" Exasperated with the clumsiness of her swollen knuckles, Wanda tore the package open and photographs spilled like a deck of cards across the table.

Gwen strolled over to fill her cup from the steaming kettle and returned, bouncing a bag of herbal tea in the water. "Fit and Fifty won't apply to me after my next birthday. I plan to propose that we change the name of the club to Sexy and Sixty."

Lifting the lid off the rooster, she spent a reverent moment contemplating the date bars inside. "Yum! Oh, your clever fingers! I can't wait to open my Christmas present and flaunt my new Wanda original."

The sincerity of her voice helped to ease the hurt and suddenly Wanda found herself telling Gwen about the phone call, her chin trembling as she repeated the cruel words that threatened to take the joy out of Christmas.

"And you with a freezer brimming with cookies and rolls." Gwen laughed, a full throated chuckle which had the same effect on the men of the Fit and Fifty as the scent of apple blossoms on honey bees. "Did you whip up a batch of your chocolate chip and pecan specials?"

Wanda found herself grinning back. "Three dozen."

Gwen scooped up two date bars and waved them under her nose with a blissful smile. "You bake like an angel kissed your fingertips, Wanda. Don't surrender a crumb of those cookies to that greedy little witch or I'll bounce you from the club!"

Wanda's smile faded. "How do you wrap money?" She shuffled through the photographs without seeing any of the colorfully costumed subjects. "I want my family to know that I love them."

"Give each of the kids a small savings bond and stiff Allyson and David," Gwen advised. "On second thought, give your son that bowling shirt you showed me. I'll bet the idea of David hobnobbing with the peasants down at the bowling alley drives your dear daughter-in-law up the wall!"

"But I want Jenny to have the skirt." A tear escaped from the hidden spring of hurt welling inside Wanda's soul and trickled down her cheek.

Gwen sobered. "That skirt is stunning. My granddaughter gets her clothes at an exclusive boutique and I'd stack up your designs against any of the ragamuffin stuff Laura wears. Fancy labels ae just for folks too blind to recognize quality."

Wanda sighed and swished the tea around in her cup.

"Allyson's not worth the misery, dearie." Gwen wrapped another date bar in a napkin and tucked it into her purse. "I've got to dash. Now, don't forget the Christmas committee meeting has been changed to Thursday. We're thinking of driving down and holding our party at that orphanage in Mexico."

She rose. "If I were any younger, I'd put one of those little charmers on my list for Santa. You won't worry about this gift thing anymore, will you?"

Wanda shook her head and pretended to sip cold tea.

That night, Wanda dreamed she was seven years old again, her feet stumbling up the steps of a sprawling, paint peeling farmhouse. Scalding tears blurred her vision; she wiped away the stinging salt with the end of a pigtail. Once again, she was dumb at spelling, too slow at recess games, and the cruel final taunts of a classmate rang in her ears.

Her grandmother was mixing biscuit dough on the maple harvester table in the kitchen. Wanda tried to slip past the doorway to seek refuge in her own room, but her grandmother's ears were keen enough to hear a mouse sneeze in the walls.

"Is that you, child? I need another scoop from the flour barrel—" She broke off and peered at her granddaughter. "Tears, Wanda? Are you ailing?"

Wanda sniffled without replying. Then, without warning the log jam of injured pride, anger, and grief broke free and the pent-up misery spilled forth. Between gulping sobs, she confessed to fleeing her tormentors. "Why did Mommy and Daddy have to die? I hate being an orphan!"

From experience, she knew that although her grandmother was generous with food and the assignment of chores, she dished out neither compliments nor sympathy with a lavish hand. Wanda was stunned into silence when the older woman led her into the parlor to the rocking chair and lifted her onto her lap, just as if she weighed no more than a babe.

For a few minutes, the only sounds were the creak of the rocker against the hardwood floor and the whistle of a mocking bird in the elm tree outside the window.

"You're my flesh and blood, Wanda," her grandmother began. "Didn't I make you this dress?"

Ducking her head, Wanda whispered assent and pleated the striped fabric of the skirt with her fingers.

The matter-of-fact voice continued. "As I sewed, I dwelt continually on how blessed we are to have you here. Whenever the other youngsters cut you with words, slip your hand into your pocket and grab a handful of the feeling put inside with each stitch. You might be the only one in your class with a pocketful of love."

Wanda opened her eyes. The sun drenched parlor, the smooth arm of the rocking chair against her back, and the yeasty scent of biscuit dough had vanished into the past, along with the gruff voice of her grandmother. She was in the present, trapped in a tiny apartment where the drip of the bathroom faucet competed with blaring music from a passing car.

Her knees throbbed. Wanda twisted the blanket and thought of Jenny. Too tall, afflicted with braces and flyaway hair Jenny. Jenny, whose mother believed that the proper application of eye shadow and the name of a 'hot' designer on the fanny of a pair of jeans guaranteed popularity.

Wanda sat up, switched on the lamp, and swung her painfully stiff leg over the side of the bed. The skirt was a warm puddle of color against the dark wood of the work table. Glancing down, she saw that one of her fists was stuffed into the pocket of her nightdress. By next year, her fingers might be too stiff for fancy sewing—and Jenny needed her now.

Knotting the cord of her dressing gown, Wanda limped into the kitchen to make her third pot of tea.

* * * *

Three weeks later, the sounds of a fiesta filled the air; shrieks of ecstatic children vied with the strumming of a guitar and strident horns.

Gwen plopped down on the bench beside Wanda and brushed strands of glittering tinsel off her shoulders. "Best party ever! Did you see those little rascals pelt me with this stuff?"

"Maybe it's that hint of green in your new hair dye that confused them. They thought you were a tree."

Gwen snorted and nudged her friend. "You sound pretty chipper for a woman who's giving savings bonds and a bowling shirt this year. Anyway, I've got a warm, tingly feeling from watching the little tykes have so much fun."

My doctor calls that sensation poor circulation," Wanda retorted with a grin.

They watched the merriment in companionable silence, moving only to pull their feet out of danger as kids hurtled past, grimy fingers clutching gift flashlights, which served as laser guns and chocolate-smeared mouths supplying graphic sound effects.

A woman whose face was worn from years of struggling to nurture the children in her care stepped forward to caution the boys to behave, but her smile as she stroked the evening cape woven with silver threads cradling her shoulders outshone the star at the top of the tree in the center of the room.

Wanda beamed back, her thoughts drifting to a skirt wrapped in gaily patterned Christmas paper, a skirt containing a designer label snipped from a dress belonging to Gwen's granddaughter. The outside of the skirt pocket was embroidered with daisies and inside was the special

Braille message of the thread bumps that Wanda would interpret for Jenny when they were alone together.

At her side, Gwen stiffened. "Is that Tom Turner doing the Mexican hat dance? He's too old for such foolishness." Springing to her feet, she stalked away, intent on rebuking such folly.

Carlos, seated on Wanda's lap, giggled. Wanda laughed with him, hugging the dark-eyed two-year-old close before brushing the crumbs of a chocolate chip and pecan cookie off the yellow duckling embroidered on his undershirt.

THE END

About the Author

Lori Ness wrote her first novel when she ran out of books that she liked to read. *Rosemary for Remembrance*, published by Harper Paperbacks under the pseudonym **Christine Arness**, was nominated for a Romantic Times Award for Best Contemporary Romantic Novel. Her second book, *Wedding Chimes, Assorted Crimes*, was a hardcover published by Five Star. She has a story in *An Old Fashioned Christmas* anthology, along with a contemporary romance, *Fairy Christmas, Darling*. Lori has also published numerous articles, short stories, newspaper articles and essays.

www.christinearness.com

www.ingramcontent.com/pod-product-compliance
Lightning Source LLC
Chambersburg PA
CBHW021125130626
46554CB00002B/861